新制多益

全新！TOEIC
聽力題庫解析
Listening

完整 10 回聽力測驗
模擬試題 MP3

單題分割 MP3

重點單字多元口音 MP3

iOS 系統請升級至 iOS13 以上版本再行下載。此為大型檔案，建議使用 Wi-Fi 連線下載，以免占用大量流量，並請確認連線狀況，以利下載順暢。

（自己的姓名）_____ 的新制多益 Listening 目標分數

_____ 分

達成日期：_____ 年 _____ 月 _____ 日

目標設定評量表

	Test 1	Test 2	Test 3	Test 4	Test 5	Test 6	Test 7	Test 8	Test 9	Test 10
495									多益高手！	
450										
400					獲得高分只是時間問題！					
350			對多益有感覺了！							
300	多益新手！									

完成各回的試題後，在上面表格的相應分數上標註 ●，以便查看自己的分數變化與進步情況。

前言

完美反映新制多益出題趨勢的
《全新！新制多益聽力題庫解析》終於出版！

　　HACKERS 出版的多益學習書系列能夠長期在暢銷排行榜上獨佔鰲頭，就是因為我們一直秉持初心，費盡心思做出更好的書，且為了反映最新出題趨勢而努力不懈。

　　為了幫助所有考生順利準備新制多益測驗，我們出版了這本完全反映實際測驗、收錄完整 10 回聽力模擬測驗的《全新！新制多益聽力題庫解析》。

徹底分析新制多益聽力測驗、讓你彷彿置身考場的完整模擬試題！

　　本書徹底分析新制多益的聽力測驗部分，收錄符合實際測驗最新題型的 10 回完整模擬試題。書中收錄的所有題型，都與新制測驗一致，且在題目本最後提供每回測驗答案紙，供考生實際練習。

　　解析部分列出各種常考題目類型並附上詳細解說及答題技巧分析。透過這樣的設計，可以讓考生確實理解之前覺得困難的題目，準備更加徹底而完整，快速提高自己的成績。

利用詳細解說以及逐題分析解題策略，幫助你獲得理想分數！

　　本書除了提供所有題目的簡答、翻譯和解析之外，也詳細剖析錯誤選項，且特別標出重點單字及發音音標，考生亦可透過收錄在解答本內的常考單字記憶表來複習及記憶單字。此外，解析中更特別針對以變換表達方式來混淆考生的題目，以「換句話說」來幫助考生熟悉經常出現在題目之中的表達方式，讓考生能確實理解題目，並逐一擊破自己的解題弱點。

　　希望這本《全新！新制多益聽力題庫解析》能夠幫助各位考生達成自己的目標分數、提升英文實力，並成為各位實踐夢想的基石。

Hackers 語言研究中心

目錄

TEST 01

Part 1

Part 2

Part 3 新

Part 4 新

自我評量表

稍等！作答前確認事項：
1. 關掉手機電源了嗎？ □是
2. 準備好答案卡、鉛筆、橡皮擦了嗎？ □是
3. 準備好聽MP3了嗎？ □是

所有準備都完成後，請先預想目標成績，把它寫在
後面的自我檢測表上，再開始作答。TEST 01 做
完後，可以評鑑自己目前的實力，並按照適合自己
的學習計畫（參看解答本 p.18~p.19），利用這本
模擬試題做有效率的學習。

📱 **TEST 01.mp3** 收錄了 **Part 1-4**。

LISTENING TEST

In this section, you must demonstrate your ability to understand spoken English. This section is divided into four parts and will take approximately 45 minutes to complete. Do not mark the answers in your test book. Use the answer sheet that is provided separately.

PART 1

Directions: For each question, you will listen to four short statements about a picture in your test book. These statements will not be printed and will only be spoken one time. Select the statement that best describes what is happening in the picture and mark the corresponding letter (A), (B), (C), or (D) on the answer sheet.

Sample Answer
Ⓐ ● Ⓒ Ⓓ

The statement that best describes the picture is (B), "The man is sitting at the desk." So, you should mark letter (B) on the answer sheet.

1.

2.

GO ON TO THE NEXT PAGE →

3.

4.

5.

6.

GO ON TO THE NEXT PAGE →

Directions: For each question, you will listen to a statement or question followed by three possible responses spoken in English. They will not be printed and will only be spoken one time. Select the best response and mark the corresponding letter (A), (B), or (C) on your answer sheet.

7. Mark your answer on your answer sheet.

8. Mark your answer on your answer sheet.

9. Mark your answer on your answer sheet.

10. Mark your answer on your answer sheet.

11. Mark your answer on your answer sheet.

12. Mark your answer on your answer sheet.

13. Mark your answer on your answer sheet.

14. Mark your answer on your answer sheet.

15. Mark your answer on your answer sheet.

16. Mark your answer on your answer sheet.

17. Mark your answer on your answer sheet.

18. Mark your answer on your answer sheet.

19. Mark your answer on your answer sheet.

20. Mark your answer on your answer sheet.

21. Mark your answer on your answer sheet.

22. Mark your answer on your answer sheet.

23. Mark your answer on your answer sheet.

24. Mark your answer on your answer sheet.

25. Mark your answer on your answer sheet.

26. Mark your answer on your answer sheet.

27. Mark your answer on your answer sheet.

28. Mark your answer on your answer sheet.

29. Mark your answer on your answer sheet.

30. Mark your answer on your answer sheet.

31. Mark your answer on your answer sheet.

PART 3

Directions: In this part, you will listen to several conversations between two or more speakers. These conversations will not be printed and will only be spoken one time. For each conversation, you will be asked to answer three questions. Select the best response and mark the corresponding letter (A), (B), (C), or (D) on your answer sheet.

32. What most likely is the man's occupation?

(A) A salesperson
(B) An accountant
(C) A lawyer
(D) A journalist

33. What does the woman say about Arnold Smith?

(A) He was recently promoted.
(B) He reported on some news.
(C) He already revised a file.
(D) He would like some advice.

34. What does the man ask the woman to do?

(A) Submit a weekly time sheet
(B) Give back a borrowed item
(C) Provide some feedback
(D) Copy some documents

35. Why is the woman calling?

(A) To request a service
(B) To make an appointment
(C) To provide directions
(D) To respond to an inquiry

36. What does the woman want to avoid doing?

(A) Taking a longer route
(B) Going to an auto repair shop
(C) Operating her vehicle
(D) Using public transportation

37. What does the man ask the woman about?

(A) Whether she reported an accident
(B) Whether she was injured in a collision
(C) Whether she arrived at a destination
(D) Whether she was notified of a situation

38. Where most likely does the man work?

(A) At a theater
(B) At a gallery
(C) At an art school
(D) At a photography studio

39. What is implied about the woman?

(A) She has contacted a famous painter.
(B) She has not had an exhibit before.
(C) She has not finished a painting.
(D) She has lived in another country.

40. When will the show most likely begin?

(A) On August 20
(B) On August 27
(C) On September 8
(D) On September 10

41. Why have the speakers been busy?

(A) A company has gotten multiple complaints.
(B) Some equipment is being installed.
(C) Some employees are being trained.
(D) A seminar took longer than expected.

42. What does Lena say recently happened?

(A) A team missed a deadline.
(B) A report was submitted.
(C) A shipment was damaged.
(D) A customer lost some data.

43. What does the man offer to do?

(A) Download a file
(B) Pay for a meal
(C) Turn in some paperwork
(D) Call a coworker

GO ON TO THE NEXT PAGE

44. What did the woman do last week?

(A) Visited an online store
(B) Requested a refund
(C) Bought some bedding
(D) Replaced a mattress

45. What does the man imply when he says, "I can look up the transaction using the number"?

(A) A purchase may be processed.
(B) A product might be available.
(C) A receipt should be located.
(D) A refund can be given.

46. What will the woman most likely do next?

(A) Find a credit card
(B) Go to another store
(C) Check a transaction fee
(D) Compare some merchandise

---

47. Where most likely is the conversation taking place?

(A) At an event hall
(B) At a fabric factory
(C) At a dry cleaner
(D) At a clothing shop

48. What does the woman suggest?

(A) Walking over to a counter
(B) Dressing in formal attire
(C) Selecting a different color
(D) Asking for another opinion

49. What will the man probably do next?

(A) Determine a wedding date
(B) Look over some expenses
(C) Find an associate
(D) Try on an item

---

50. What problem does the man mention?

(A) A concert has been canceled.
(B) A venue was unexpectedly closed.
(C) A show experienced technical difficulties.
(D) A band did not appear as planned.

51. What did the man do yesterday?

(A) Viewed some comments
(B) Visited a ticketing office
(C) Checked schedule changes
(D) Submitted a complaint

52. Why does the woman say, "we can provide you with a 20 percent discount"?

(A) To promote a service
(B) To recommend an option
(C) To fulfill a request
(D) To confirm a choice

---

53. What are the speakers mainly discussing?

(A) Making an applicant list
(B) Creating a job advertisement
(C) Choosing a candidate
(D) Arranging a training session

54. What is Jamie currently working on?

(A) A sales report
(B) A meeting agenda
(C) A consumer survey
(D) A marketing study

55. What will the woman probably do after the meeting?

(A) Contact an applicant
(B) Conduct an interview
(C) Edit a posting
(D) Listen to a voice mail

---

56. What does the man suggest?

    (A) Reviewing educational materials
    (B) Changing degree requirements
    (C) Funding professional development
    (D) Updating hiring procedures

57. According to the woman, what took place last Friday?

    (A) A charity event
    (B) A business seminar
    (C) A press conference
    (D) An executive meeting

58. What does the woman ask the man to do?

    (A) Call some directors
    (B) Research some amounts
    (C) Find a training program
    (D) Meet with a financial consultant

59. Why does the woman place the call?

    (A) To verify warranty information
    (B) To complain about an error
    (C) To ask about a return policy
    (D) To place a product order

60. Why does the woman say, "it will be a gift for her housewarming party"?

    (A) To confirm a delivery time
    (B) To ask for a different service
    (C) To provide a reason for a request
    (D) To express concern about a delay

61. What will the man probably do next?

    (A) Shut down a system
    (B) Input order details
    (C) Meet with shipping personnel
    (D) Cancel a previous charge

62. Where most likely is the conversation taking place?

    (A) At a product launch
    (B) At a business conference
    (C) At a shareholders' meeting
    (D) At a trade fair

63. How is this year's event different from the previous one?

    (A) More funding was used.
    (B) Registration fees are higher.
    (C) More attendees are present.
    (D) Additional space was created.

64. What has the man promised to do?

    (A) Take over a work shift
    (B) Set up a booth
    (C) Replace some equipment
    (D) Distribute some documents

GO ON TO THE NEXT PAGE

Holly's Cake Shop Menu

Type	Size	Price
Coconut Cake	8 in	$36
Strawberry Cheesecake	10 in	$54
Carrot Cake	12 in	$46
Chocolate Cake	14 in	$58

65. Why does the woman thank the man?

(A) He gave her a venue recommendation.
(B) He helped her move to a new office.
(C) He surprised her with a gift.
(D) He reminded her of an occasion.

66. What does the man propose doing?

(A) Using a meeting space
(B) Browsing a sample menu
(C) Choosing a special decoration
(D) Increasing a price limit

67. Look at the graphic. Which cake will the man order?

(A) Coconut Cake
(B) Strawberry Cheesecake
(C) Carrot Cake
(D) Chocolate Cake

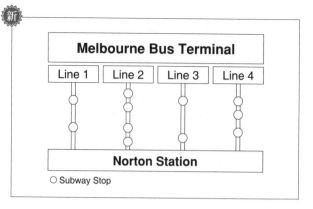

68. Where most likely does the man work?

(A) At a transportation authority
(B) At a travel agency
(C) At an electronics producer
(D) At a cosmetics retailer

69. What does the woman ask about?

(A) The location of an item
(B) The reliability of a service
(C) The time of a delivery
(D) The duration of an event

70. Look at the graphic. Which subway line did the woman take today?

(A) Line 1
(B) Line 2
(C) Line 3
(D) Line 4

PART 4

Directions: In this part, you will listen to several short talks by a single speaker. These talks will not be printed and will only be spoken one time. For each talk, you will be asked to answer three questions. Select the best response and mark the corresponding letter (A), (B), (C), or (D) on your answer sheet.

71. What did the speaker agree to do?

    (A) Attend an event
    (B) Carpool to a meeting
    (C) Distribute an itinerary
    (D) Organize a festival

72. What will happen at 6:30 on Saturday?

    (A) A park will close.
    (B) A band will be interviewed.
    (C) A reservation will be made.
    (D) A performance will begin.

73. What does the speaker want to do later today?

    (A) Exchange a product
    (B) Purchase some tickets
    (C) Visit a venue
    (D) Send some invitations

74. What is the problem?

    (A) A client has made a complaint.
    (B) A device does not function.
    (C) A discount is no longer available.
    (D) A competitor is offering a new service.

75. What does the speaker mention about the Web site?

    (A) It includes additional features.
    (B) It will be updated regularly.
    (C) It was launched yesterday.
    (D) It is receiving fewer visitors.

76. What does the speaker imply when she says, "Our prices are already low"?

    (A) She is upset with a coworker.
    (B) She is doubtful about an idea.
    (C) She is confused by a situation.
    (D) She is concerned about a budget.

77. What is the speaker advertising?

    (A) A speaker system
    (B) A kitchen appliance
    (C) A device operator
    (D) A television set

78. According to the speaker, how is EX3 different from competing products?

    (A) It is more durable.
    (B) It uses fewer batteries.
    (C) It comes in more colors.
    (D) It is easier to use.

79. What will customers receive if they register a product online?

    (A) A reduced price
    (B) A complimentary item
    (C) A gift card
    (D) An extended warranty

80. What did the speaker recently do?

    (A) Placed a product order
    (B) Contacted a new supplier
    (C) Called a delivery person
    (D) Canceled a purchase

81. What does the speaker imply when he says, "I really can't believe it"?

    (A) He is shocked by a guest turnout.
    (B) He is worried about a late shipment.
    (C) He is overwhelmed with requests.
    (D) He is disappointed with a service.

82. What is suggested about The Blue House Restaurant's grand opening?

    (A) It was delayed.
    (B) It began at noon.
    (C) It had few attendees.
    (D) It included free beverages.

GO ON TO THE NEXT PAGE

83. Where most likely is the speaker?

(A) At a shopping center
(B) In an engineering office
(C) At a construction site
(D) In a radio station

84. What are listeners advised to do?

(A) Postpone a trip
(B) Avoid traveling downtown
(C) Take public transportation
(D) Check traffic conditions

85. What will most likely happen next?

(A) An alternative route will be described.
(B) An interview will be conducted.
(C) An accident location will be identified.
(D) An event schedule will be announced.

86. What is the purpose of the call?

(A) To cancel a funds transfer
(B) To verify an online payment
(C) To request an account number
(D) To report a security measure

87. What problem does the speaker mention?

(A) A daily limit was exceeded.
(B) Transactions were made in two cities.
(C) A banking service was unavailable.
(D) Several purchases were made at a store.

88. What does the speaker recommend the listener do?

(A) Examine a record
(B) Make a withdrawal
(C) Visit a center
(D) Change a password

89. What is the announcement mainly about?

(A) Employee training
(B) An updated evaluation system
(C) Customer feedback
(D) A new company policy

90. When do security personnel arrive at the building?

(A) At 7:00 A.M.
(B) At 7:30 A.M.
(C) At 8:00 A.M.
(D) At 8:30 A.M.

91. What does the speaker say he will do this afternoon?

(A) Alter a schedule
(B) Revise a manual
(C) Hand out a document
(D) Give a presentation

新	Mon	Tue	Wed	Thu
9 A.M. – 11 A.M.		Session 2	Session 3	
2 P.M. – 4 P.M.	Session 1			Session 4

92. Who most likely is the speaker?

(A) A writer
(B) An actor
(C) A cameraperson
(D) A director

93. Look at the graphic. When will the speaker and Nancy Davis attend a session together?

(A) Monday
(B) Tuesday
(C) Wednesday
(D) Thursday

94. What is included in the e-mail sent by the speaker?

(A) Details about a role
(B) Assignments for a team
(C) Requests from a producer
(D) Changes to a script

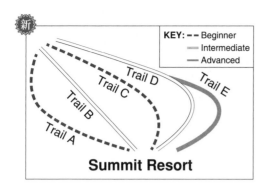

Summit Resort

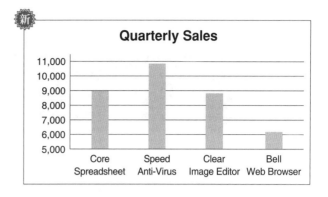

95. What will the listeners do first?

(A) Practice snowboarding techniques
(B) Go to the resort's lobby
(C) Read a safety manual
(D) Watch an instructional video

96. Why should listeners go to the second floor of the building?

(A) To pay for some lessons
(B) To rent a room
(C) To meet a teacher
(D) To get some equipment

97. Look at the graphic. Which trail will the listeners use?

(A) Trail A
(B) Trail B
(C) Trail C
(D) Trail D

98. What department do the listeners most likely work in?

(A) Sales
(B) Marketing
(C) Accounting
(D) Human resources

99. Look at the graphic. Which software product will the company stop selling?

(A) Core Spreadsheet
(B) Speed Anti-Virus
(C) Clear Image Editor
(D) Bell Web Browser

100. What does the speaker ask the listeners to do?

(A) Submit a report
(B) Test a product
(C) Download a program
(D) Prepare a proposal

解答 p.146 / 分數換算表 p.149 / 題目解析 p.21（解答本）

▌請翻到次頁的「自我檢測表」檢視自己解答問題的方法與態度。
▌請利用 p.149 分數換算表換算完分數後，請翻至解答本的 p.18~p.19 查看適合自己的學習計畫，並請確實實踐。

自我檢測表

順利結束 TEST 01 了嗎？

現在透過以下問題來檢視一下自己的作答情況吧！

1. 我在作答時，中間沒有停下來過。

   □ 是　□ 否

   若答案為否，理由是為什麼呢？

2. 我有確實劃記答案紙上的每一道題目。

   □ 是　□ 否

   若答案為否，理由是為什麼呢？

3. 作答 Part 2 的 25 題時，我非常專心於題目上。

   □ 是　□ 否

   若答案為否，理由是為什麼呢？

4. 作答 Part 3 時，我在聽題目音檔前都已先看過題目和選項。

   □ 是　□ 否

   若答案為否，理由是為什麼呢？

5. 作答 Part 4 時，我在聽題目音檔前都已先看過題目和選項。

   □ 是　□ 否

   若答案為否，理由是為什麼呢？

6. 請寫下需要改進之處或給自己的建議。

★請確認自己在進行作答前寫下的目標分數，並再次堅定要達成目標的決心。需要改進的地方務必
　於下一回測驗中實踐，這一點非常重要，唯有如此才能更進步。

TEST 02

Part 1

Part 2

Part 3 新

Part 4 新

自我評量表

稍等！作答前確認事項：
1. 關掉手機電源了嗎？ □是
2. 準備好答案卡、鉛筆、橡皮擦了嗎？ □是
3. 準備好聽MP3了嗎？ □是

所有準備都完成後，請先預想目標成績，把它寫在
後面的自我檢測表上，再開始作答。

📱 **TEST 02.mp3** 收錄了 **Part 1-4**。

LISTENING TEST

In this section, you must demonstrate your ability to understand spoken English. This section is divided into four parts and will take approximately 45 minutes to complete. Do not mark the answers in your test book. Use the answer sheet that is provided separately.

PART 1

Directions: For each question, you will listen to four short statements about a picture in your test book. These statements will not be printed and will only be spoken one time. Select the statement that best describes what is happening in the picture and mark the corresponding letter (A), (B), (C), or (D) on the answer sheet.

Sample Answer
Ⓐ ● Ⓒ Ⓓ

The statement that best describes the picture is (B), "The man is sitting at the desk." So, you should mark letter (B) on the answer sheet.

1.

2.

GO ON TO THE NEXT PAGE ➡

3.

4.

5.

6.

GO ON TO THE NEXT PAGE ➡

PART 2

Directions: For each question, you will listen to a statement or question followed by three possible responses spoken in English. They will not be printed and will only be spoken one time. Select the best response and mark the corresponding letter (A), (B), or (C) on your answer sheet.

7.   Mark your answer on your answer sheet.

8.   Mark your answer on your answer sheet.

9.   Mark your answer on your answer sheet.

10. Mark your answer on your answer sheet.

11. Mark your answer on your answer sheet.

12. Mark your answer on your answer sheet.

13. Mark your answer on your answer sheet.

14. Mark your answer on your answer sheet.

15. Mark your answer on your answer sheet.

16. Mark your answer on your answer sheet.

17. Mark your answer on your answer sheet.

18. Mark your answer on your answer sheet.

19. Mark your answer on your answer sheet.

20. Mark your answer on your answer sheet.

21. Mark your answer on your answer sheet.

22. Mark your answer on your answer sheet.

23. Mark your answer on your answer sheet.

24. Mark your answer on your answer sheet.

25. Mark your answer on your answer sheet.

26. Mark your answer on your answer sheet.

27. Mark your answer on your answer sheet.

28. Mark your answer on your answer sheet.

29. Mark your answer on your answer sheet.

30. Mark your answer on your answer sheet.

31. Mark your answer on your answer sheet.

PART 3

Directions: In this part, you will listen to several conversations between two or more speakers. These conversations will not be printed and will only be spoken one time. For each conversation, you will be asked to answer three questions. Select the best response and mark the corresponding letter (A), (B), (C), or (D) on your answer sheet.

32. What will the community center receive?

(A) Donations from a company
(B) Computers from local charities
(C) Funds from the government
(D) Equipment from a university

33. What are the speakers planning to do?

(A) Upgrade old devices
(B) Move to a larger building
(C) Order additional books
(D) Run an educational workshop

34. Why must the speakers review some documents?

(A) To compare some prices
(B) To identify some donors
(C) To determine some restrictions
(D) To research some venues

35. Why did the woman contact the man?

(A) To verify a delivery time
(B) To inquire about job duties
(C) To arrange an interview
(D) To confirm a contract detail

36. When will the speakers most likely meet?

(A) On Thursday morning
(B) On Thursday afternoon
(C) On Friday morning
(D) On Friday afternoon

37. What will the man most likely bring for the woman?

(A) A résumé
(B) A work sample
(C) An application form
(D) A reference letter

38. What does the man say about Detroit?

(A) It experienced bad weather.
(B) It has a newly built airport.
(C) It is only an hour away.
(D) It is hosting a major event.

39. According to the woman, why is Mr. Herman coming to the office?

(A) To train some personnel
(B) To discuss travel arrangements
(C) To make an announcement
(D) To observe a presentation

40. What will the man probably do next?

(A) Take a lunch break
(B) Begin a meeting
(C) Pass on some information
(D) Share some sales reports

41. What problem does the woman mention?

(A) A line has formed at a device.
(B) A machine has been damaged.
(C) A bank has closed for construction.
(D) A fee has been increased.

42. What does the woman mean when she says, "I'm in a bit of a rush"?

(A) She needs to return to the office.
(B) She does not want to miss a train.
(C) She has to catch a flight soon.
(D) She is late for a social gathering.

43. What does the man suggest the woman do?

(A) Make a formal complaint
(B) Travel to another branch
(C) Postpone a trip
(D) Speak with an employee

GO ON TO THE NEXT PAGE

44. According to the woman, what has caused a distraction?

(A) Excessive heat
(B) Building construction
(C) Untidy offices
(D) Noisy appliances

45. What does the woman ask the man to do?

(A) Replace some equipment
(B) Send a technician
(C) Clean an office space
(D) Change an appointment date

46. What is probably going to take place on Friday?

(A) A company outing
(B) A retirement party
(C) A technical seminar
(D) A grand opening

47. Where does the woman work?

(A) At a consultancy
(B) At a real estate company
(C) At a grocery store
(D) At a landscaping firm

48. What does the woman say her company did last summer?

(A) Took on a commercial job
(B) Expanded to other cities
(C) Relocated its headquarters
(D) Raised its prices

49. What does the woman ask for?

(A) Property locations
(B) Budget amounts
(C) Price comparisons
(D) Project details

50. What is the purpose of the woman's visit?

(A) To view some test results
(B) To schedule an appointment
(C) To get some medication
(D) To pick up a building map

51. Who most likely are the men?

(A) Pharmacists
(B) Doctors
(C) Medical researchers
(D) Clinic directors

52. What information does Daniel provide?

(A) The location for a shot
(B) The name of a business
(C) The cost of an examination
(D) The number of a room

53. When will a meeting take place?

(A) In one day
(B) In two days
(C) In three days
(D) In four days

54. What does the woman want to do?

(A) Speak with a department head
(B) Set a project timeline
(C) Practice giving a presentation
(D) Attend a technology conference

55. What does the man mean when he says, "I can join you in the conference room"?

(A) He will finish a task soon.
(B) He will offer some comments.
(C) He has agreed to a time change.
(D) He has booked a meeting space.

56. Where most likely are the speakers?

(A) In a building lobby
(B) At a real estate office
(C) At a construction site
(D) In a residential unit

57. Why does the woman want to wait to make up her mind?

(A) She needs to determine a budget.
(B) She has to consult a friend.
(C) She will look at another space.
(D) She is unsure about contract terms.

58. What happened earlier today?

(A) An open house event was advertised.
(B) A vacant apartment was visited.
(C) A property was professionally cleaned.
(D) A down payment was made.

---

59. What is the conversation mainly about?

(A) The reason for evaluations
(B) The details of a negotiation
(C) The success of an investment
(D) The cost of operations

60. What is mentioned about staff?

(A) They will receive salary increases.
(B) They will learn specialized skills.
(C) They will transfer to a new division.
(D) They will undergo an assessment.

61. Why does the woman require the man's approval?

(A) She needs to conduct an analysis.
(B) She plans to post a memo.
(C) She wants to submit another offer.
(D) She wishes to agree to a deal.

Area A	Area B
Refreshment Stand	
Area C	Area D
Entrance	

62. What type of event is happening tonight?

(A) A performance rehearsal
(B) An awards ceremony
(C) A movie screening
(D) A play opening

63. What does the woman ask the man to do?

(A) Arrange some furniture
(B) Work a late shift
(C) Hang up some frames
(D) Greet incoming guests

64. Look at the graphic. Where most likely will photos be taken?

(A) In Area A
(B) In Area B
(C) In Area C
(D) In Area D

GO ON TO THE NEXT PAGE

Pacific Sports Supplies

20% off any purchase over $100

Valid until July 31
At all branches in California
May be combined with other discounts

Flight	Destination	Status	Updated Arrival Time
AB701	Phoenix	On Time	9:00 A.M.
UR770	Portland	Delayed	10:30 A.M.
WX803	Cincinnati	Delayed	12:00 P.M.
ZP890	Portland	On Time	3:30 P.M.
TA900	Dallas	Delayed	6:00 P.M.

65. What does the man ask about?

(A) The popularity of some merchandise
(B) The durability of a component
(C) The weight of some equipment
(D) The availability of an accessory

66. Look at the graphic. Why is the man unable to use the coupon?

(A) An expiration date has already passed.
(B) A branch is not participating in a promotion.
(C) A product is currently on sale.
(D) A purchase amount is too low.

67. What will the woman probably do next?

(A) Provide gear recommendations
(B) Restock a bike display
(C) Lead a customer to a checkout
(D) Process a request for a refund

68. Why is the man worried?

(A) A ticket was not printed.
(B) An airport is located far away.
(C) A flight might be missed.
(D) A terminal has been blocked off.

69. What does the man want to do?

(A) Listen to a lecture on a laptop
(B) Access the Internet
(C) Check in at a gate
(D) Inform a supervisor of an arrival time

70. Look at the graphic. Which flight will the speakers take?

(A) UR770
(B) WX803
(C) ZP890
(D) TA900

PART 4

Directions: In this part, you will listen to several short talks by a single speaker. These talks will not be printed and will only be spoken one time. For each talk, you will be asked to answer three questions. Select the best response and mark the corresponding letter (A), (B), (C), or (D) on your answer sheet.

71. What was changed recently?

   (A) The name of a company
   (B) The time of an appointment
   (C) The cost of a service
   (D) The location of a business

72. What is the listener asked to do?

   (A) Request new glasses
   (B) Contact a physician
   (C) Arrange an examination
   (D) Bring a document

73. Why should the listener show up early?

   (A) To talk with a specialist
   (B) To pay an outstanding bill
   (C) To complete some paperwork
   (D) To take a short test

74. What is mentioned about the Eastwood Entertainment?

   (A) It is planning a fundraiser.
   (B) It has recently relocated.
   (C) It will hire a new manager.
   (D) It purchased a venue.

75. What does the speaker imply when he says, "tickets will go quickly"?

   (A) A theater has few seats.
   (B) A deal is ending.
   (C) A price is reasonable.
   (D) An actor is famous.

76. What does the speaker recommend that listeners do?

   (A) View an online map
   (B) Purchase a discounted ticket
   (C) Attend a press conference
   (D) Call a local theater

77. Who is the speaker?

   (A) A research assistant
   (B) A corporate advisor
   (C) A product engineer
   (D) A Web site designer

78. What did the speaker do five years ago?

   (A) Started a new company
   (B) Created a social media platform
   (C) Oversaw a business merger
   (D) Accepted a job at an agency

79. What will happen over the next two weeks?

   (A) Discounts will be offered.
   (B) A survey will be conducted.
   (C) A campaign will be developed.
   (D) Evaluations will be performed.

80. What type of business is being advertised?

   (A) An electronics retailer
   (B) A waste disposal company
   (C) An appliance repair shop
   (D) A computer manufacturer

81. According to the speaker, what happens each month?

   (A) A device is put on sale.
   (B) An exhibit is held.
   (C) An item is given away.
   (D) A donation is made.

82. How can listeners take part in a drawing?

   (A) By becoming a member
   (B) By making an online profile
   (C) By using a coupon
   (D) By spending a certain amount

GO ON TO THE NEXT PAGE

83. Where most likely does the speaker work?

(A) At a university
(B) At a print shop
(C) At a financial firm
(D) At an advertising agency

84. Why are volunteers needed?

(A) To plan a job fair for students
(B) To rent an informational booth
(C) To post flyers around a city
(D) To represent a business at an event

85. According to the speaker, what has already been done?

(A) A legal professional was contacted.
(B) Some handouts were prepared.
(C) Applications were collected.
(D) Some questions were answered.

86. What are the listeners working on this week?

(A) Designing an electronic device
(B) Preparing for a trade show
(C) Organizing a corporate workshop
(D) Developing a software program

87. What does the speaker imply when he says, "I'm even willing to give you an extra day to finish up your project"?

(A) A machine still needs to be fixed.
(B) A team has too few personnel.
(C) A training session is important.
(D) A lot of problems have been found.

88. What does the speaker recommend?

(A) Registering for an event
(B) Meeting with superiors
(C) Reviewing a program
(D) Conducting a study

89. What is the purpose of the call?

(A) To cancel a payment
(B) To change a service
(C) To confirm an address
(D) To make a complaint

90. What does the speaker mean when she says, "I think he needs to visit my home again"?

(A) A package was not delivered.
(B) A worker was not available.
(C) A treatment was not effective.
(D) A task was not agreed upon.

91. What does the speaker want to discuss?

(A) An application process
(B) A refund policy
(C) A future appointment
(D) A discount amount

92. What is the topic of the seminar?

(A) Labor laws
(B) Trade regulations
(C) Investment strategies
(D) Overseas markets

93. What will most likely happen first?

(A) A case study will be reviewed.
(B) Guests will divide into groups.
(C) Programs will be handed out.
(D) A talk will be given.

94. According to the speaker, what will listeners be able to do?

(A) Work on independent exercises
(B) Inquire about their fields
(C) Take a brief break for lunch
(D) Turn in forms after the session

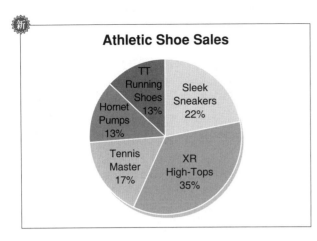

Athletic Shoe Sales

TT Running Shoes 13%	Sleek Sneakers 22%
Hornet Pumps 13%	
Tennis Master 17%	XR High-Tops 35%

Animal Name	Species	Age
Mocha	Sand fox	5 months
Ginger	Jackal	10 months
Omar	Hyena	6 years
Pebble	Ostrich	28 years

95. Who most likely is the speaker?

(A) A product designer
(B) A company spokesperson
(C) A research analyst
(D) A corporate lawyer

96. What did the speaker do last week?

(A) Held an informal meeting
(B) Distributed questionnaires
(C) Responded to queries
(D) Tested merchandise

97. Look at the graphic. Which product are customers dissatisfied with?

(A) XR High-Tops
(B) Sleek Sneakers
(C) Tennis Master
(D) Hornet Pumps

98. Who most likely are the listeners?

(A) Guest lecturers
(B) Government inspectors
(C) New employees
(D) University students

99. What is mentioned about the Sahara Wildlife Reserve?

(A) It relies entirely on donations.
(B) It will be expanded this year.
(C) It offers internship opportunities.
(D) It cannot take in any more animals.

100. Look at the graphic. What will the listeners see first?

(A) A sand fox
(B) A jackal
(C) A hyena
(D) An ostrich

解答 **p.146** / 分數換算表 **p.149** / 題目解析 **p.65**（解答本）

▌請翻到次頁的「自我檢測表」檢視自己解答問題的方法與態度。
▌請利用 **p.149** 分數換算表換算完分數。

自我檢測表

順利結束 TEST 02 了嗎？

現在透過以下問題來檢視一下自己的作答情況吧！

1. 我在作答時，中間沒有停下來過。

   □ 是　□ 否

   若答案為否，理由是為什麼呢？

2. 我有確實劃記答案紙上的每一道題目。

   □ 是　□ 否

   若答案為否，理由是為什麼呢？

3. 作答 Part 2 的 25 題時，我非常專心於題目上。

   □ 是　□ 否

   若答案為否，理由是為什麼呢？

4. 作答 Part 3 時，我在聽題目音檔前都已先看過題目和選項。

   □ 是　□ 否

   若答案為否，理由是為什麼呢？

5. 作答 Part 4 時，我在聽題目音檔前都已先看過題目和選項。

   □ 是　□ 否

   若答案為否，理由是為什麼呢？

6. 請寫下需要改進之處或給自己的建議。

★請確認自己在進行作答前寫下的目標分數，並再次堅定要達成目標的決心。需要改進的地方務必於下一回測驗中實踐，這一點非常重要，唯有如此才能更進步。

TEST 03

Part 1

Part 2

Part 3 新

Part 4 新

自我評量表

稍等！作答前確認事項：
1. 關掉手機電源了嗎？ □是
2. 準備好答案卡、鉛筆、橡皮擦了嗎？ □是
3. 準備好聽MP3了嗎？ □是

所有準備都完成後，請先預想目標成績，把它寫在
後面的自我檢測表上，再開始作答。

📢 **TEST 03.mp3** 收錄了 **Part 1-4**。

LISTENING TEST

In this section, you must demonstrate your ability to understand spoken English. This section is divided into four parts and will take approximately 45 minutes to complete. Do not mark the answers in your test book. Use the answer sheet that is provided separately.

PART 1

Directions: For each question, you will listen to four short statements about a picture in your test book. These statements will not be printed and will only be spoken one time. Select the statement that best describes what is happening in the picture and mark the corresponding letter (A), (B), (C), or (D) on the answer sheet.

Sample Answer
Ⓐ ● Ⓒ Ⓓ

The statement that best describes the picture is (B), "The man is sitting at the desk." So, you should mark letter (B) on the answer sheet.

1.

2.

GO ON TO THE NEXT PAGE ➤

3.

4.

5.

6.

GO ON TO THE NEXT PAGE ➡

PART 2

Directions: For each question, you will listen to a statement or question followed by three possible responses spoken in English. They will not be printed and will only be spoken one time. Select the best response and mark the corresponding letter (A), (B), or (C) on your answer sheet.

7. Mark your answer on your answer sheet.

8. Mark your answer on your answer sheet.

9. Mark your answer on your answer sheet.

10. Mark your answer on your answer sheet.

11. Mark your answer on your answer sheet.

12. Mark your answer on your answer sheet.

13. Mark your answer on your answer sheet.

14. Mark your answer on your answer sheet.

15. Mark your answer on your answer sheet.

16. Mark your answer on your answer sheet.

17. Mark your answer on your answer sheet.

18. Mark your answer on your answer sheet.

19. Mark your answer on your answer sheet.

20. Mark your answer on your answer sheet.

21. Mark your answer on your answer sheet.

22. Mark your answer on your answer sheet.

23. Mark your answer on your answer sheet.

24. Mark your answer on your answer sheet.

25. Mark your answer on your answer sheet.

26. Mark your answer on your answer sheet.

27. Mark your answer on your answer sheet.

28. Mark your answer on your answer sheet.

29. Mark your answer on your answer sheet.

30. Mark your answer on your answer sheet.

31. Mark your answer on your answer sheet.

PART 3

Directions: In this part, you will listen to several conversations between two or more speakers. These conversations will not be printed and will only be spoken one time. For each conversation, you will be asked to answer three questions. Select the best response and mark the corresponding letter (A), (B), (C), or (D) on your answer sheet.

32. Who most likely are the speakers?

(A) Travel agents
(B) Event planners
(C) Advertising executives
(D) Environmental researchers

33. What is mentioned about the Silkwood Hotel?

(A) It launched a new service.
(B) It has renovated its suites.
(C) It is hosting a conference.
(D) It will hold a promotion.

34. What does the man ask the woman to do?

(A) Call a company
(B) Make a reservation
(C) Revise a newsletter
(D) Send an e-mail

35. Where most likely do the speakers work?

(A) At a car rental agency
(B) At a home electronics shop
(C) At a furniture retailer
(D) At a courier company

36. Why is the man worried?

(A) More vehicles may be required.
(B) Customers have submitted complaints.
(C) Branches might be closed.
(D) Total sales have dropped.

37. What does the woman ask for?

(A) An electronic device
(B) A truck key
(C) An order form
(D) A business card

38. What is the conversation mainly about?

(A) A company dinner
(B) A guest list
(C) A remodeling project
(D) A customer survey

39. What does the woman recommend?

(A) Speaking to a manager
(B) Training some staff
(C) Changing some rules
(D) Attending a conference

40. What did the man do last week?

(A) Sampled a food selection
(B) Hired a new chef
(C) Participated in an event
(D) Modified an agenda

41. What problem does the woman mention?

(A) A worker is not available.
(B) An inspection was rescheduled.
(C) A bill has not arrived.
(D) A charge was higher than expected.

42. What does the woman imply when she says, "It could be a big job"?

(A) She is concerned about cost.
(B) She would like to get another opinion.
(C) She will hire an assistant.
(D) She thinks a project should be postponed.

43. What will the man probably do next?

(A) Replace a broken pipe
(B) Provide contact information
(C) Look for a cheaper alternative
(D) Order additional tools

GO ON TO THE NEXT PAGE

44. What is the conversation mainly about?

(A) A printing error
(B) A construction project
(C) A business pamphlet
(D) An employee transfer

45. What happened last month?

(A) Customer refunds were processed.
(B) A new location was opened.
(C) An agreement was signed.
(D) Some facilities were renovated.

46. What does the man offer to do?

(A) Distribute some brochures
(B) Inspect a building
(C) Interview a designer
(D) Contact another company

47. What does the woman ask the man about?

(A) A deadline extension
(B) A project's progress
(C) A staff request
(D) A meeting's location

48. Why does the woman say, "It seems like the right thing to do"?

(A) To approve an employee transfer
(B) To recommend hosting a celebration
(C) To show support for higher salaries
(D) To promote a potential candidate

49. What does the man suggest?

(A) Postponing a client appointment
(B) Mentioning a proposal at a gathering
(C) Finishing presentation materials
(D) Rearranging seats for a conference

50. What is the problem?

(A) A purchase was not approved.
(B) A delivery will arrive late.
(C) A device is malfunctioning.
(D) A proposal was rejected.

51. What is scheduled to happen in the afternoon?

(A) An employee orientation
(B) An executive meeting
(C) A technology seminar
(D) A product demonstration

52. What does the man imply about the IT department?

(A) It will hire additional staff.
(B) It is not currently busy.
(C) It moved to a new office.
(D) It has a new department head.

53. According to the woman, what do some customers want to buy?

(A) A portable charger
(B) A room furnishing
(C) A mobile phone
(D) A remote controller

54. What is the man uncertain about?

(A) Why a product is unavailable
(B) Where an item is located
(C) How much a device costs
(D) When a shipment will arrive

55. What does the woman suggest?

(A) Assigning another worker to a shift
(B) Offering customers a discount
(C) Contacting a product manufacturer
(D) Rewarding some staff members

56. How did the woman find out about the event at the museum?

(A) By listening to the radio
(B) By watching television
(C) By reading a magazine
(D) By talking to a friend

57. According to the man, what did the National Space Agency do?

(A) Purchased some instruments
(B) Conducted a study
(C) Designed a display
(D) Provided some items

58. What costs an extra fee?

(A) Participating in a guided tour
(B) Accessing a temporary exhibit
(C) Attending a lecture series
(D) Viewing a documentary film

59. What does the man ask the woman about?

(A) The location of merchandise
(B) Preparations for an event
(C) The progress of construction work
(D) Plans for a staff meeting

60. According to the man, when do the extra racks need to arrive?

(A) On Tuesday
(B) On Wednesday
(C) On Thursday
(D) On Friday

61. What does the man say he will do?

(A) Sweep the aisles
(B) Verify supply levels
(C) Confirm a discount amount
(D) Locate delivered packages

62. According to the man, what did the woman do earlier today?

(A) Recorded a message
(B) Stopped by a reception desk
(C) Received a parcel
(D) Canceled an order

63. What does the woman mean when she says, "That's what I figured"?

(A) She noticed an error.
(B) She confirmed a delay.
(C) She anticipated a cost increase.
(D) She identified staffing needs.

64. When did the man originally plan to finish the work?

(A) At 10 A.M.
(B) At 11 A.M.
(C) At 12 P.M.
(D) At 1 P.M.

GO ON TO THE NEXT PAGE

Bedford Dry Cleaners

Customer: Paula Steinman

Drop-off Date: May 22

Item	Service	Charge
Jean jacket	Add buttons	$5
Silk dress	Shorten	$15
Leather skirt	Clean	$20
Silk shirt	Press	$10
Total Paid		$50

Hartford Public Library
New Books (August)

Field	Title	Available from
Language	*Beginner Japanese*	August 7
Home	*Storage and You*	August 7
History	*The History of London*	August 13
Travel	*A Guide to Marseilles*	August 13

65. What event will the speakers attend tomorrow night?

(A) A grand opening sale
(B) A fashion show
(C) A fund-raising event
(D) A trade fair

66. Why does the man want to switch dry cleaners?

(A) A garment was damaged.
(B) A business is going to close.
(C) A promotion has expired.
(D) A location is more convenient.

67. Look at the graphic. Which service qualifies for a discount?

(A) Adding buttons
(B) Shortening
(C) Cleaning
(D) Pressing

68. According to the man, what is the maximum loan period?

(A) One week
(B) Two weeks
(C) Three weeks
(D) Four weeks

69. Look at the graphic. Which book will arrive in September?

(A) *Beginner Japanese*
(B) *Storage and You*
(C) *The History of London*
(D) *A Guide to Marseilles*

70. What will the man most likely do next?

(A) Update a library account
(B) Search for a publication
(C) Order a replacement book
(D) Speak with a supervisor

PART 4

Directions: In this part, you will listen to several short talks by a single speaker. These talks will not be printed and will only be spoken one time. For each talk, you will be asked to answer three questions. Select the best response and mark the corresponding letter (A), (B), (C), or (D) on your answer sheet.

71. What can employees do next week?
(A) Sign up for a contest
(B) Donate some items
(C) Make various crafts
(D) Decorate a lobby

72. When will employees most likely visit the community center?
(A) On June 9
(B) On June 12
(C) On June 13
(D) On June 16

73. What should some listeners do before the end of the day?
(A) Contact a coworker
(B) Pick up a product
(C) Participate in a workshop
(D) Request a deadline extension

74. What is the speaker mainly discussing?
(A) A damaged product
(B) An overdue rental
(C) A new return policy
(D) An online reservation

75. What does the speaker recommend the listener do on the holidays?
(A) Use the side entrance of a building
(B) Call an information hotline
(C) Place an item in a container
(D) Go to the shop in the morning

76. Why should the listener act quickly?
(A) A schedule has been changed.
(B) A complaint has been made.
(C) A service will be canceled.
(D) An amount will increase.

77. Who most likely is Mark Campbell?
(A) An actor
(B) A tour guide
(C) A resort manager
(D) A photographer

78. Why does the speaker say, "We'll spend about an hour here"?
(A) To request that listeners be patient
(B) To encourage participation in a performance
(C) To notify listeners of a schedule change
(D) To confirm that a plan will be followed

79. What are listeners instructed to do?
(A) Keep their shoes on
(B) Avoid touching a display
(C) Secure their belongings
(D) Use protective gear

80. What happened yesterday?
(A) A retail facility began operations.
(B) A construction site was chosen.
(C) An economic report was released.
(D) A company merger took place.

81. What does the speaker say about the city government?
(A) It will request repayment of a debt.
(B) It will receive additional revenue.
(C) It will take control of a property.
(D) It will manage a renovation project.

82. What is suggested about Analytic Systems?
(A) It will increase its payroll taxes.
(B) It will purchase another factory.
(C) Its relocation caused many job losses.
(D) Its closure was due to financial problems.

GO ON TO THE NEXT PAGE

83. Who most likely is the speaker?

(A) A caterer
(B) A hotel manager
(C) A decorator
(D) A conference organizer

84. What does the man mean when he says, "A real triumph"?

(A) A company has won an award.
(B) A task was difficult to complete.
(C) A request was unexpected.
(D) An event was well attended.

85. What will the man do later in the day?

(A) Prepare a budget
(B) Answer some questions
(C) E-mail a client
(D) Send some samples

86. What is the purpose of the announcement?

(A) To promote a product
(B) To announce a regulation
(C) To describe an event
(D) To introduce a service

87. What does the speaker mention about the device?

(A) It can be used in many museums.
(B) It plays content automatically.
(C) It must be reserved in advance.
(D) It has several language settings.

88. According to the speaker, how can listeners get information about a temporary exhibition?

(A) By speaking to an employee
(B) By visiting a booth
(C) By joining a group
(D) By reading a pamphlet

89. What is being advertised?

(A) A television package
(B) An insurance policy
(C) An Internet service
(D) An electronic device

90. What do residents qualify for?

(A) A gift certificate
(B) A software upgrade
(C) A discounted rate
(D) A complimentary trial

91. What should listeners bring to the office?

(A) A copy of a receipt
(B) A credit card
(C) A registration form
(D) A piece of identification

Delivery Schedule		
Date	Company	Shipment Contents
May 12	Lloyd Ferris	Dishwashers
May 13	Monroe Industries	Dryers
May 14	Abdul & Sons	Microwaves
May 15	Stone Incorporated	Refrigerators

92. Where do the listeners work?

(A) At a retail store
(B) At a distribution center
(C) At a testing facility
(D) At a manufacturing plant

93. What does the speaker ask one of the listeners to do?

(A) Give an employee a tour
(B) Post a notice near an exit
(C) Print out a new schedule
(D) Record some notes

94. Look at the graphic. Which company has postponed its delivery?

(A) Lloyd Ferris
(B) Monroe Industries
(C) Abdul & Sons
(D) Stone Incorporated

Oakridge Subway Station

Exit 10 Harbor Street	Exit 11 Field Street
Exit 12 Bridge Street	Exit 13 Oak Street

Leung Kitchen	Thayer Technologies		Patsy's Diner
Parking Lot	Westside Supermarket	Gray Road	
Cedar Street			
Hayden Park	Luis Pizzeria		Shea Pub
	Parking Lot		

95. Why is the speaker calling?

(A) To announce an art gallery opening
(B) To explain a membership program
(C) To notify a prize winner
(D) To request an outstanding payment

96. What does the speaker offer to do?

(A) Exchange some tickets
(B) Cancel a fee
(C) Provide a refund
(D) Reserve some seats

97. Look at the graphic. Which exit is closest to the administration office?

(A) Exit 10
(B) Exit 11
(C) Exit 12
(D) Exit 13

98. According to the speaker, what did the interns do?

(A) Assisted with a company event
(B) Participated in off-site training
(C) Organized a surprise party
(D) Created a financial report

99. What are the listeners told to do?

(A) Cancel a team meeting
(B) Submit a project plan
(C) Conduct intern evaluations
(D) Reschedule overtime work

100. Look at the graphic. Where does the speaker suggest going?

(A) Leung Kitchen
(B) Patsy's Diner
(C) Luis Pizzeria
(D) Shea Pub

解答 **p.146** / 分數換算表 **p.149** / 題目解析 **p.109**（解答本）

▌請翻到次頁的「自我檢測表」檢視自己解答問題的方法與態度。
▌請利用 **p.149** 分數換算表換算完分數。

LISTENING

1 2 3 4 5 6 7 8 9 10

自我檢測表

順利結束 TEST 03 了嗎？

現在透過以下問題來檢視一下自己的作答情況吧！

1. 我在作答時，中間沒有停下來過。

   ☐ 是　☐ 否

   若答案為否，理由是為什麼呢？

2. 我有確實劃記答案紙上的每一道題目。

   ☐ 是　☐ 否

   若答案為否，理由是為什麼呢？

3. 作答 Part 2 的 25 題時，我非常專心於題目上。

   ☐ 是　☐ 否

   若答案為否，理由是為什麼呢？

4. 作答 Part 3 時，我在聽題目音檔前都已先看過題目和選項。

   ☐ 是　☐ 否

   若答案為否，理由是為什麼呢？

5. 作答 Part 4 時，我在聽題目音檔前都已先看過題目和選項。

   ☐ 是　☐ 否

   若答案為否，理由是為什麼呢？

6. 請寫下需要改進之處或給自己的建議。

★請確認自己在進行作答前寫下的目標分數，並再次堅定要達成目標的決心。需要改進的地方務必
於下一回測驗中實踐，這一點非常重要，唯有如此才能更進步。

TEST 04

Part 1

Part 2

Part 3 新

Part 4 新

自我評量表

稍等！作答前確認事項：
1. 關掉手機電源了嗎？ □是
2. 準備好答案卡、鉛筆、橡皮擦了嗎？ □是
3. 準備好聽MP3了嗎？ □是

所有準備都完成後，請先預想目標成績，把它寫在後面的自我檢測表上，再開始作答。

TEST 04.mp3 收錄了 Part 1-4。

LISTENING TEST

In this section, you must demonstrate your ability to understand spoken English. This section is divided into four parts and will take approximately 45 minutes to complete. Do not mark the answers in your test book. Use the answer sheet that is provided separately.

PART 1

Directions: For each question, you will listen to four short statements about a picture in your test book. These statements will not be printed and will only be spoken one time. Select the statement that best describes what is happening in the picture and mark the corresponding letter (A), (B), (C), or (D) on the answer sheet.

Sample Answer
Ⓐ ● Ⓒ Ⓓ

The statement that best describes the picture is (B), "The man is sitting at the desk." So, you should mark letter (B) on the answer sheet.

1.

2.

GO ON TO THE NEXT PAGE →

3.

4.

5.

6.

GO ON TO THE NEXT PAGE ➤

PART 2

Directions: For each question, you will listen to a statement or question followed by three possible responses spoken in English. They will not be printed and will only be spoken one time. Select the best response and mark the corresponding letter (A), (B), or (C) on your answer sheet.

7.   Mark your answer on your answer sheet.

8.   Mark your answer on your answer sheet.

9.   Mark your answer on your answer sheet.

10. Mark your answer on your answer sheet.

11. Mark your answer on your answer sheet.

12. Mark your answer on your answer sheet.

13. Mark your answer on your answer sheet.

14. Mark your answer on your answer sheet.

15. Mark your answer on your answer sheet.

16. Mark your answer on your answer sheet.

17. Mark your answer on your answer sheet.

18. Mark your answer on your answer sheet.

19. Mark your answer on your answer sheet.

20. Mark your answer on your answer sheet.

21. Mark your answer on your answer sheet.

22. Mark your answer on your answer sheet.

23. Mark your answer on your answer sheet.

24. Mark your answer on your answer sheet.

25. Mark your answer on your answer sheet.

26. Mark your answer on your answer sheet.

27. Mark your answer on your answer sheet.

28. Mark your answer on your answer sheet.

29. Mark your answer on your answer sheet.

30. Mark your answer on your answer sheet.

31. Mark your answer on your answer sheet.

PART 3

Directions: In this part, you will listen to several conversations between two or more speakers. These conversations will not be printed and will only be spoken one time. For each conversation, you will be asked to answer three questions. Select the best response and mark the corresponding letter (A), (B), (C), or (D) on your answer sheet.

32. What is the conversation mainly about?
    (A) A new telephone system
    (B) A technical issue
    (C) A departmental meeting
    (D) A building renovation

33. What is Mr. Bradford's team doing?
    (A) Fixing an Intranet system
    (B) Bringing in more materials
    (C) Repairing some telephone lines
    (D) Establishing a wireless connection

34. What does the woman suggest?
    (A) Working on a different floor
    (B) Unplugging a machine from the wall
    (C) Notifying customers about an error
    (D) Purchasing a piece of equipment

35. What does the man's family plan to do?
    (A) Book a table at a restaurant
    (B) Find some accommodations
    (C) Travel to another country
    (D) Visit a tourist attraction

36. What is provided for free to guests?
    (A) Meals
    (B) Internet access
    (C) Transportation
    (D) Guidebooks

37. Why does the woman ask the man to wait?
    (A) She needs to help someone else.
    (B) She needs to verify something.
    (C) She wants to provide a brochure.
    (D) She wants to print passes to a site.

38. Who most likely is the man?
    (A) A performer
    (B) An event planner
    (C) An instructor
    (D) A radio host

39. What is mentioned about the Carter Institute?
    (A) It organizes lessons for musicians.
    (B) It receives support from the city.
    (C) It holds performances for children.
    (D) It gives funds to local groups.

40. What does the woman mean when she says, "we have a special treat for listeners"?
    (A) A ticket will be given away.
    (B) A special guest will be introduced.
    (C) An interview will be held.
    (D) A musical piece will be played.

41. What are the speakers mainly discussing?
    (A) A press conference
    (B) An architect position
    (C) A photo shoot
    (D) A magazine subscription

42. What does the woman propose?
    (A) Meeting at a construction site
    (B) Rescheduling an appointment
    (C) Contacting a theater owner
    (D) Revising an article

43. What does the man say the woman can do?
    (A) Return to a venue at a later date
    (B) Bring a copy of a publication
    (C) Exhibit some images at a gallery
    (D) Print out some blueprints

GO ON TO THE NEXT PAGE

44. According to the woman, what happened last Tuesday?

(A) A professional contract expired.
(B) A shipment of goods arrived.
(C) A complaint was submitted online.
(D) A customer exchanged an item.

45. How does the man want to deal with the problem?

(A) By renewing an agreement
(B) By demanding a full refund
(C) By starting a new business relationship
(D) By asking for a membership discount

46. What does the woman request the man do?

(A) Display some signs
(B) Organize a storage area
(C) Edit a service catalog
(D) Deliver some merchandise

47. What is the conversation mainly about?

(A) Expenses for a billboard design
(B) The length of a marketing campaign
(C) Materials for a business presentation
(D) The results of a periodic evaluation

48. What does the man suggest the woman do?

(A) Replace some images
(B) Delegate duties to workers
(C) Perform market research
(D) Include more information

49. What will the woman emphasize?

(A) The types of products being released
(B) The reaction of people to different colors
(C) The cost of organizing a focus group
(D) The success of a television commercial

50. Where do the speakers most likely work?

(A) At a financial institution
(B) At a staffing agency
(C) At an office supply store
(D) At a graphic design firm

51. What did Tim and Laura do this morning?

(A) Met with a potential client
(B) Attended a staff meeting
(C) Made travel arrangements
(D) Conducted job interviews

52. What do Tim and Laura recommend?

(A) Reviewing a contract
(B) Visiting some companies
(C) Explaining some benefits
(D) Changing a process

53. Who most likely is Joowon Kim?

(A) A technician
(B) A Web designer
(C) A company intern
(D) An accountant

54. Why does the man say, "He'll use it for the budget analysis project"?

(A) To extend an assignment deadline
(B) To inform a manager of a change
(C) To advocate for more training
(D) To emphasize the necessity of a task

55. What will the woman probably do next?

(A) Log on to a system
(B) Contact another team
(C) Read a financial report
(D) Revise a service request

56. What problem does the woman mention?

(A) She forgot to update an application.
(B) A machine stopped functioning.
(C) She is unfamiliar with a program.
(D) An inventory level is too low.

57. What does the man suggest?

(A) Referring to a handbook
(B) E-mailing some colleagues
(C) Consulting with an advisor
(D) Copying some manuals

58. According to the man, what should the woman talk to the manager about?

(A) Acquiring additional computer parts
(B) Customizing some new software
(C) Errors in an important file
(D) Complications with a messaging system

59. Why is the man calling the woman?

(A) To discuss a potential inaccuracy
(B) To report a computer glitch
(C) To switch a payment method
(D) To announce staff replacements

60. What does the woman say about Teresa Ford?

(A) She was transferred to another department.
(B) She has been assigned additional hours.
(C) She is using the wrong time sheets.
(D) She needs to submit some documents.

61. What will the woman probably do next?

(A) Take a call from a customer
(B) Update employee payroll records
(C) Submit a request to a coworker
(D) Analyze some sales data

Eastside Cable				
	Service			
	Premium Sports Channels	Game Downloads	Premium Movie Channels	Video Recording
Package A	√		√	√
Package B		√		√
Package C	√	√	√	

62. What did the man forget?

(A) An activation code
(B) A product pamphlet
(C) A fee payment
(D) A visit time

63. Look at the graphic. Which service is the man most interested in?

(A) Premium Sports Channels
(B) Game Downloads
(C) Premium Movie Channels
(D) Video Recording

64. According to the woman, what is the man unable to receive?

(A) A gift with purchase
(B) A company brochure
(C) A piece of equipment
(D) A reduced price

GO ON TO THE NEXT PAGE

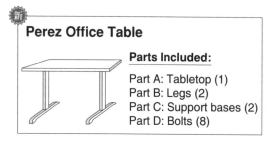

Perez Office Table

Parts Included:

Part A: Tabletop (1)
Part B: Legs (2)
Part C: Support bases (2)
Part D: Bolts (8)

65. Where does the conversation most likely take place?

(A) In a meeting room
(B) In an employee lounge
(C) In a furniture store
(D) In a warehouse

66. Look at the graphic. Which part is missing?

(A) Part A
(B) Part B
(C) Part C
(D) Part D

67. What will the man probably do during his lunch break?

(A) Call a business
(B) Move some tables
(C) Look over a manual
(D) Find additional tools

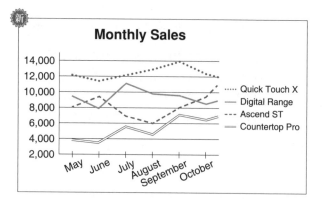

Monthly Sales

..... Quick Touch X
— Digital Range
--- Ascend ST
— Countertop Pro

68. Why did the woman miss the event?

(A) She was welcoming new employees.
(B) She was leading a department workshop.
(C) She was talking to an executive.
(D) She was meeting with a client.

69. Look at the graphic. Which model will the woman give a presentation on?

(A) Quick Touch X
(B) Digital Range
(C) Ascend ST
(D) Countertop Pro

70. What does the man offer to do?

(A) Organize an investor event
(B) Gather some information
(C) Help with a marketing campaign
(D) Edit a sales report

PART 4

Directions: In this part, you will listen to several short talks by a single speaker. These talks will not be printed and will only be spoken one time. For each talk, you will be asked to answer three questions. Select the best response and mark the corresponding letter (A), (B), (C), or (D) on your answer sheet.

71. Who most likely is the speaker?
    (A) A delivery person
    (B) A tow truck driver
    (C) A hospital employee
    (D) A city worker

72. What does the speaker remind listeners to do?
    (A) Use marked entrances and exits
    (B) Consult with medical officials
    (C) Contact emergency personnel
    (D) Avoid parking in certain zones

73. According to the speaker, what should listeners look for?
    (A) Detour signs
    (B) Colored lines
    (C) Lighted displays
    (D) Traffic cones

74. Why does the speaker say, "there's a massive snowstorm here"?
    (A) To express concern about a delivery
    (B) To request help with booking a flight
    (C) To indicate uncertainty about a decision
    (D) To provide the reason for a delay

75. According to the speaker, what did the listener do last year?
    (A) He helped develop a program.
    (B) He hired a programmer.
    (C) He gave a presentation to a client.
    (D) He transferred to another branch.

76. What does the speaker suggest the listener do?
    (A) Reschedule a meeting
    (B) Speak with an assistant
    (C) Cancel a trip
    (D) E-mail a file

77. According to the speaker, what will happen in August?
    (A) Some computers will be purchased.
    (B) A division will be expanded.
    (C) A building will be renovated.
    (D) Some workers will be trained.

78. What is located on the fourth floor?
    (A) Temporary workstations
    (B) Executive offices
    (C) Construction tools
    (D) New conference rooms

79. What will most likely be done toward the end of this month?
    (A) Desks will be set up.
    (B) Equipment will be moved.
    (C) Staff will go on leave.
    (D) Painters will finish a job.

80. Where most likely does the speaker work?
    (A) At a real estate firm
    (B) At a retail outlet
    (C) At a travel agency
    (D) At a delivery company

81. What does the speaker instruct the listener to do?
    (A) Provide an electronic signature
    (B) Return a parcel
    (C) Visit a facility
    (D) Confirm an address

82. What does the speaker say might happen after seven days?
    (A) A message will be sent out.
    (B) A request will be processed.
    (C) A tracking number will expire.
    (D) A package will be shipped back.

GO ON TO THE NEXT PAGE

83. What is the speaker mainly discussing?

   (A) A company expansion
   (B) A performance incentive
   (C) An upcoming promotion
   (D) A budget increase

84. Who is the speaker most likely addressing?

   (A) Corporate executives
   (B) Event organizers
   (C) Hotel personnel
   (D) Sales professionals

85. What does the speaker mean when she says, "that still wasn't good enough"?

   (A) An employee achieved better results.
   (B) A task was not completed on schedule.
   (C) A contract will have to be revised.
   (D) A team must participate in a program.

---

86. What type of business most likely is Digital Solutions?

   (A) An online retailer
   (B) A software developer
   (C) A graphic design company
   (D) A recording studio

87. Why has the firm's stock value risen?

   (A) Its product has been very successful.
   (B) Its operations have moved overseas.
   (C) It was awarded a major contract.
   (D) It has teamed up with another business.

88. What does the speaker say will happen next month?

   (A) A device will be distributed to stores.
   (B) A merger will be formalized.
   (C) An application will be released.
   (D) A cell phone will be reviewed.

89. According to the speaker, what did the company recently do?

   (A) Launched a new service
   (B) Closed some offices
   (C) Joined with another firm
   (D) Changed some policies

90. What will probably happen in October?

   (A) Personnel will begin working.
   (B) A team will be assembled.
   (C) A department will be shut down.
   (D) Employees will create a database.

91. What does the speaker imply when he says, "The marketing team isn't able to access some records"?

   (A) A task will be reassigned.
   (B) A job should not be postponed.
   (C) A supervisor should be notified.
   (D) A project will be canceled.

---

92. Why is the speaker calling?

   (A) To ask about an incorrect invoice
   (B) To change an earlier order
   (C) To thank a company for its services
   (D) To get information about a speaker

93. What does Music Central need?

   (A) Extra microphones
   (B) A partial refund
   (C) Additional speakers
   (D) An extended warranty

94. What is the listener asked to do this afternoon?

   (A) Send a revised statement
   (B) Print a company catalog
   (C) Fill out a registration form
   (D) Ship a sample product

Survey Results	
Air Conditioner	34%
Air Purifier	26%
Electric Fan	22%
Space Heater	18%

95. Why is Greg Henderson unavailable?

(A) He is participating in a focus group.
(B) He is attending a design conference.
(C) He is visiting a production plant.
(D) He is inspecting a research facility.

96. Look at the graphic. What type of device is the Flow S60?

(A) An air conditioner
(B) An air purifier
(C) An electric fan
(D) A space heater

97. What will the speaker distribute?

(A) Manuals
(B) Application forms
(C) Promotional brochures
(D) Questionnaires

Bean Bus Tour

Departure	Boston Common
Stop 1	Newbury Street
Stop 2	Boston Harbor
Stop 3	Old State House
Stop 4	Bunker Hill

98. What does the speaker mention about the information booth?

(A) It opened five years ago.
(B) It will begin selling souvenirs.
(C) It has few employees.
(D) It is located in a hotel.

99. Which month will the company offer a discount?

(A) April
(B) May
(C) June
(D) July

100. Look at the graphic. Which stop will be temporarily inaccessible?

(A) Stop 1
(B) Stop 2
(C) Stop 3
(D) Stop 4

解答 p.146 / 分數換算表 p.149 / 題目解析 p.153（解答本）

❚ 請翻到次頁的「自我檢測表」檢視自己解答問題的方法與態度。
❚ 請利用 p.149 分數換算表換算完分數。

LISTENING

1 2 3 4 5 6 7 8 9 10

自我檢測表

順利結束 TEST 04 了嗎？

現在透過以下問題來檢視一下自己的作答情況吧！

1. 我在作答時，中間沒有停下來過。

   ☐ 是　☐ 否

   若答案為否，理由是為什麼呢？

2. 我有確實劃記答案紙上的每一道題目。

   ☐ 是　☐ 否

   若答案為否，理由是為什麼呢？

3. 作答 Part 2 的 25 題時，我非常專心於題目上。

   ☐ 是　☐ 否

   若答案為否，理由是為什麼呢？

4. 作答 Part 3 時，我在聽題目音檔前都已先看過題目和選項。

   ☐ 是　☐ 否

   若答案為否，理由是為什麼呢？

5. 作答 Part 4 時，我在聽題目音檔前都已先看過題目和選項。

   ☐ 是　☐ 否

   若答案為否，理由是為什麼呢？

6. 請寫下需要改進之處或給自己的建議。

★請確認自己在進行作答前寫下的目標分數，並再次堅定要達成目標的決心。需要改進的地方務必
　於下一回測驗中實踐，這一點非常重要，唯有如此才能更進步。

TEST 05

Part 1

Part 2

Part 3 新

Part 4 新

自我評量表

稍等！作答前確認事項：
1. 關掉手機電源了嗎？ □是
2. 準備好答案卡、鉛筆、橡皮擦了嗎？ □是
3. 準備好聽MP3了嗎？ □是

所有準備都完成後，請先預想目標成績，把它寫在後面的自我檢測表上，再開始作答。

🎧 **TEST 05.mp3** 收錄了 **Part 1-4**。

LISTENING TEST

In this section, you must demonstrate your ability to understand spoken English. This section is divided into four parts and will take approximately 45 minutes to complete. Do not mark the answers in your test book. Use the answer sheet that is provided separately.

PART 1

Directions: For each question, you will listen to four short statements about a picture in your test book. These statements will not be printed and will only be spoken one time. Select the statement that best describes what is happening in the picture and mark the corresponding letter (A), (B), (C), or (D) on the answer sheet.

Sample Answer
Ⓐ ● Ⓒ Ⓓ

The statement that best describes the picture is (B), "The man is sitting at the desk." So, you should mark letter (B) on the answer sheet.

1.

2.

GO ON TO THE NEXT PAGE →

3.

4.

5.

6.

GO ON TO THE NEXT PAGE

PART 2

Directions: For each question, you will listen to a statement or question followed by three possible responses spoken in English. They will not be printed and will only be spoken one time. Select the best response and mark the corresponding letter (A), (B), or (C) on your answer sheet.

7.   Mark your answer on your answer sheet.

8.   Mark your answer on your answer sheet.

9.   Mark your answer on your answer sheet.

10. Mark your answer on your answer sheet.

11. Mark your answer on your answer sheet.

12. Mark your answer on your answer sheet.

13. Mark your answer on your answer sheet.

14. Mark your answer on your answer sheet.

15. Mark your answer on your answer sheet.

16. Mark your answer on your answer sheet.

17. Mark your answer on your answer sheet.

18. Mark your answer on your answer sheet.

19. Mark your answer on your answer sheet.

20. Mark your answer on your answer sheet.

21. Mark your answer on your answer sheet.

22. Mark your answer on your answer sheet.

23. Mark your answer on your answer sheet.

24. Mark your answer on your answer sheet.

25. Mark your answer on your answer sheet.

26. Mark your answer on your answer sheet.

27. Mark your answer on your answer sheet.

28. Mark your answer on your answer sheet.

29. Mark your answer on your answer sheet.

30. Mark your answer on your answer sheet.

31. Mark your answer on your answer sheet.

PART 3

Directions: In this part, you will listen to several conversations between two or more speakers. These conversations will not be printed and will only be spoken one time. For each conversation, you will be asked to answer three questions. Select the best response and mark the corresponding letter (A), (B), (C), or (D) on your answer sheet.

32. Why is the man calling?

(A) To purchase a ticket
(B) To hire a car service
(C) To change a reservation
(D) To confirm a flight time

33. Where will Ms. Ming most likely go first upon arrival?

(A) To an office
(B) To a train station
(C) To a hotel
(D) To a rental agency

34. What does the woman say she will do?

(A) Update a timetable
(B) Sign an agreement
(C) Return a vehicle
(D) Wait in an airport

35. What are the speakers mainly discussing?

(A) Local restaurants
(B) Food rates
(C) Event catering
(D) Diet programs

36. What does the woman mention about the menu?

(A) It includes a vegetarian selection.
(B) It was recently revised.
(C) It indicates discounts for group orders.
(D) It shows new drink varieties.

37. What does the woman ask the man about?

(A) Meal prices
(B) Venue choices
(C) Delivery times
(D) Beverage options

38. Who most likely is the woman?

(A) A clinic patient
(B) A personal assistant
(C) A receptionist
(D) A pharmacist

39. What does the woman ask for?

(A) An insurance card
(B) A driver's license
(C) A registration form
(D) A medicine prescription

40. According to the woman, what is a benefit of the new system?

(A) Patients will be notified.
(B) Records will be protected.
(C) Information will be shared.
(D) Software will be upgraded.

41. What is the purpose of the call?

(A) To arrange a workshop tour
(B) To order some decorative items
(C) To reserve an exhibition booth
(D) To propose a business deal

42. What does the woman offer to do?

(A) Visit a store
(B) Mail some samples
(C) Reduce some prices
(D) Hang up a frame

43. What does the man ask about?

(A) A production capacity
(B) The size of a workforce
(C) A manufacturing process
(D) The names of some assistants

GO ON TO THE NEXT PAGE

44. According to the woman, what does the supervisor want to do?

(A) Search for an architect
(B) Change a meeting time
(C) Look over some plans
(D) Evaluate some staff

45. What problem does the man mention?

(A) A task is taking too long.
(B) A new hire is going to be late.
(C) A building has been closed down.
(D) A customer has made a complaint.

46. Why does the man say, "I'll e-mail you the presentation materials in a minute"?

(A) To agree to take on an assignment
(B) To show interest in a project
(C) To accept an offer of help
(D) To express concern about a situation

---

47. What are the speakers mainly discussing?

(A) A museum closing
(B) A historical site
(C) A remodeled venue
(D) A future exhibition

48. What does Brian imply about Hall C?

(A) It is currently vacant.
(B) It will be expanded soon.
(C) It is bigger than another area.
(D) It will be used for a convention.

49. Why is the woman concerned?

(A) A project deadline is unclear.
(B) A display has too few items.
(C) A space has to be enlarged.
(D) A schedule might be tight.

---

50. What did the woman do last week?

(A) Finished taking a class
(B) Completed an accounting report
(C) Attended a ceremony
(D) Taught a business course

51. What does the man ask the woman to do?

(A) Seek out an advisor
(B) Check some messages
(C) Rearrange a schedule
(D) Respond to some questions

52. What will the man probably do after 2 P.M.?

(A) Get in touch with the woman again
(B) Distribute handouts to participants
(C) Visit an administrator's office
(D) Submit a curriculum outline

---

53. Who most likely is the woman?

(A) A supermarket manager
(B) A restaurant owner
(C) A produce vendor
(D) A market analyst

54. What does the man mean when he says, "My blog gets a lot of visitors"?

(A) A Web site needs to be updated.
(B) An information source is accurate.
(C) An online discount is available.
(D) An advertising method is effective.

55. What will the woman probably do next?

(A) Request a product sample
(B) Sell some merchandise
(C) Look over some research
(D) Speak to an event organizer

---

56. What is scheduled to take place tomorrow?

(A) A trade fair
(B) A private party
(C) A corporate event
(D) A community festival

57. According to the man, what has the woman agreed to do?

(A) Pass out programs to guests
(B) Arrive in the afternoon
(C) Set up some booths
(D) Manage ticket sales

58. What does the man ask the woman to do?

(A) Contribute to a charity
(B) Replace another worker
(C) Revise some records
(D) Coordinate with a supervisor

59. Where do the speakers most likely work?

(A) At a gallery
(B) At a spa
(C) At a design studio
(D) At a retail outlet

60. Why does the woman say, "Don't we have something like that near the entrance"?

(A) To propose a solution
(B) To confirm a location
(C) To offer encouragement
(D) To disagree with a suggestion

61. What does the woman suggest?

(A) Looking for artwork online
(B) Picking up a catalog
(C) Taking an extended break
(D) Going to a popular attraction

62. What type of business do the speakers probably work for?

(A) A taxi service
(B) A vehicle rental agency
(C) A shipping company
(D) An automotive dealership

63. What does the woman propose?

(A) Asking a worker to make a delivery
(B) Meeting a customer at a main office
(C) Changing some travel arrangements
(D) Contacting a different location

64. What does the man request?

(A) A notification upon arrival
(B) A ride to another facility
(C) A prepayment for a reservation
(D) A duplicate of an agreement

GO ON TO THE NEXT PAGE

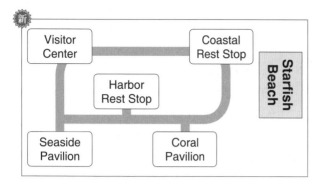

65. Look at the graphic. Where is the observation deck located?

(A) In Seaside Pavilion
(B) In Coastal Rest Stop
(C) In Harbor Rest Stop
(D) In Coral Pavilion

66. What does the woman say about the boardwalk?

(A) It will be crowded tomorrow.
(B) It will undergo renovations.
(C) It is far from a parking lot.
(D) It was damaged by poor weather.

67. How much of a parking fee discount is offered to local residents?

(A) 10 percent
(B) 15 percent
(C) 20 percent
(D) 25 percent

Conference Room C Schedule	
Meeting Time	Booked By
10 A.M. – 11 A.M.	Scott White
1 P.M. – 2 P.M.	Vera Gonzalez
3 P.M. – 4 P.M.	Brad Derby
4 P.M. – 5 P.M.	Janice Chung

68. What problem does the woman mention?

(A) A meeting space is fully booked.
(B) A mark has been made on a rug.
(C) An applicant is running behind schedule.
(D) A light fixture has been damaged.

69. Look at the graphic. Who booked the room for a client meeting?

(A) Scott White
(B) Vera Gonzalez
(C) Brad Derby
(D) Janice Chung

70. What will the man probably do next?

(A) Collect some documents
(B) Contact a colleague
(C) Attend an interview
(D) Download some information

PART 4

Directions: In this part, you will listen to several short talks by a single speaker. These talks will not be printed and will only be spoken one time. For each talk, you will be asked to answer three questions. Select the best response and mark the corresponding letter (A), (B), (C), or (D) on your answer sheet.

71. Where does the speaker most likely work?

(A) At a financial institution
(B) At a recruitment firm
(C) At a sportswear retailer
(D) At a chain restaurant

72. How much of a discount can some customers receive?

(A) 5 percent
(B) 10 percent
(C) 15 percent
(D) 20 percent

73. What is the listener instructed to do?

(A) Call a hotline
(B) Complete an online form
(C) Reset an old code
(D) Learn about a point system

74. What is the purpose of the speech?

(A) To introduce an employee
(B) To provide instructions
(C) To open a conference
(D) To promote a new car

75. According to the speaker, what was Mr. Chao in charge of?

(A) Writing a magazine article
(B) Communicating with clients
(C) Meeting monthly sales targets
(D) Running an advertising campaign

76. What has the company done recently?

(A) Cut its production costs
(B) Opened a new branch
(C) Increased its earnings
(D) Launched a publication

77. What is the announcement mainly about?

(A) A store opening
(B) A membership upgrade
(C) A monthly sale
(D) An event promotion

78. What does the speaker say people will be excited to do?

(A) Attend a screening
(B) Sign up for a newsletter
(C) Watch a performance
(D) Meet an author

79. What does the speaker suggest listeners do?

(A) Purchase a pass
(B) Download a program
(C) Check an online schedule
(D) Bring a valid ID card

80. What industry does the speaker most likely work in?

(A) Manufacturing
(B) Construction
(C) Advertising
(D) Distribution

81. Why does the speaker say, "Elevated Time sells its watches in over 50 countries"?

(A) To motivate some volunteers
(B) To emphasize the growth of a company
(C) To encourage registration
(D) To highlight the significance of a deal

82. What does the speaker expect to do?

(A) Make an upcoming deadline
(B) Expand a factory
(C) Continue a business relationship
(D) Develop a successful design

GO ON TO THE NEXT PAGE

83. Who most likely is the speaker?

(A) A political candidate
(B) A journalist
(C) A private attorney
(D) A government employee

84. What was the speaker responsible for?

(A) Overseeing an expansion
(B) Creating regulations
(C) Managing a special budget
(D) Carrying out research

85. What does the speaker say about the party?

(A) He expected more guests.
(B) He did not know about it.
(C) He planned to invite his family.
(D) He was involved in organizing it.

---

86. Where most likely are the listeners?

(A) At a university
(B) At an outdoor market
(C) At a sports facility
(D) At a community park

87. Why does the speaker say, "That area must be kept clear for emergency vehicles"?

(A) To explain a request
(B) To correct a misstatement
(C) To make a complaint
(D) To suggest an alternative

88. What are listeners asked to do after the event?

(A) Clean up a venue
(B) Assist attendees
(C) Speak with a staff member
(D) Direct traffic

---

89. According to the speaker, what will be opening this week?

(A) A toy shop
(B) A radio station
(C) An artist workspace
(D) An apartment building

90. What is mentioned about Wentworth Warehouse?

(A) It was converted into housing.
(B) It was purchased at a discount.
(C) It was demolished recently.
(D) It was moved to another area.

91. What will listeners probably hear next?

(A) A song
(B) An advertisement
(C) A news report
(D) An interview

Landville Plaza Directory	
Floor	Department
1	Finance
2	Sales
3	Human Resources
4	Customer Service
5	Research and Development

92. According to the speaker, what did the listener do yesterday?

(A) Held interviews with applicants
(B) Departed for a gathering
(C) Talked to a colleague
(D) Transferred to a new division

93. What is Victoria Styles willing to do?

(A) Lead an orientation session
(B) Accept a promotion
(C) Make some travel arrangements
(D) Reach out to a customer

94. Look at the graphic. What department does Victoria Styles work in?

(A) Finance
(B) Human Resources
(C) Customer Service
(D) Research and Development

EASTERN FERRY LINE

ADULT
SINGLE FARE

Destination: Hartsville
Ship Name: Atlantic Star

Ticket No. E12304

Monday	Tuesday	Wednesday	Thursday	Friday
☔	☀	☔	☀	☀

95. Look at the graphic. When will the ticket holder be permitted to board the vessel?

(A) At 3:10 P.M.
(B) At 3:30 P.M.
(C) At 4:00 P.M.
(D) At 4:10 P.M.

96. What is the cause of the delay?

(A) A vehicle broke down.
(B) A tow truck is unavailable.
(C) A ship must be inspected.
(D) A ferry has been overbooked.

97. What are listeners asked to do?

(A) Reserve a seat
(B) Read a document
(C) Exchange a ticket
(D) Check a schedule

98. Why does the speaker thank the listeners?

(A) A feature was added to a product.
(B) A model received positive reviews.
(C) A report contained accurate data.
(D) A task was finished ahead of schedule.

99. Look at the graphic. When will the test most likely be conducted?

(A) On Tuesday
(B) On Wednesday
(C) On Thursday
(D) On Friday

100. What did Charlotte Cruz do this morning?

(A) Confirmed a reservation
(B) Contacted another department
(C) Inspected a site
(D) Set up some equipment

解答 **p.147** / 分數換算表 **p.149** / 題目解析 **p.197**（解答本）

▍請翻到次頁的「自我檢測表」檢視自己解答問題的方法與態度。
▍請利用 **p.149** 分數換算表換算完分數。

自我檢測表

順利結束 TEST 05 了嗎？

現在透過以下問題來檢視一下自己的作答情況吧！

1. 我在作答時，中間沒有停下來過。

   ☐ 是　☐ 否

   若答案為否，理由是為什麼呢？

2. 我有確實劃記答案紙上的每一道題目。

   ☐ 是　☐ 否

   若答案為否，理由是為什麼呢？

3. 作答 Part 2 的 25 題時，我非常專心於題目上。

   ☐ 是　☐ 否

   若答案為否，理由是為什麼呢？

4. 作答 Part 3 時，我在聽題目音檔前都已先看過題目和選項。

   ☐ 是　☐ 否

   若答案為否，理由是為什麼呢？

5. 作答 Part 4 時，我在聽題目音檔前都已先看過題目和選項。

   ☐ 是　☐ 否

   若答案為否，理由是為什麼呢？

6. 請寫下需要改進之處或給自己的建議。

★請確認自己在進行作答前寫下的目標分數，並再次堅定要達成目標的決心。需要改進的地方務必於下一回測驗中實踐，這一點非常重要，唯有如此才能更進步。

TEST 06

Part 1

Part 2

Part 3 新

Part 4 新

自我評量表

稍等！作答前確認事項：
1. 關掉手機電源了嗎？ □是
2. 準備好答案卡、鉛筆、橡皮擦了嗎？ □是
3. 準備好聽MP3了嗎？ □是

所有準備都完成後，請先預想目標成績，把它寫在
後面的自我檢測表上，再開始作答。

🎧 **TEST 06.mp3** 收錄了 **Part 1-4**。

LISTENING TEST

In this section, you must demonstrate your ability to understand spoken English. This section is divided into four parts and will take approximately 45 minutes to complete. Do not mark the answers in your test book. Use the answer sheet that is provided separately.

PART 1

Directions: For each question, you will listen to four short statements about a picture in your test book. These statements will not be printed and will only be spoken one time. Select the statement that best describes what is happening in the picture and mark the corresponding letter (A), (B), (C), or (D) on the answer sheet.

Sample Answer
Ⓐ ● Ⓒ Ⓓ

The statement that best describes the picture is (B), "The man is sitting at the desk." So, you should mark letter (B) on the answer sheet.

1.

2.

GO ON TO THE NEXT PAGE ⟶

3.

4.

5.

6.

GO ON TO THE NEXT PAGE ➡

PART 2

Directions: For each question, you will listen to a statement or question followed by three possible responses spoken in English. They will not be printed and will only be spoken one time. Select the best response and mark the corresponding letter (A), (B), or (C) on your answer sheet.

7. Mark your answer on your answer sheet.

8. Mark your answer on your answer sheet.

9. Mark your answer on your answer sheet.

10. Mark your answer on your answer sheet.

11. Mark your answer on your answer sheet.

12. Mark your answer on your answer sheet.

13. Mark your answer on your answer sheet.

14. Mark your answer on your answer sheet.

15. Mark your answer on your answer sheet.

16. Mark your answer on your answer sheet.

17. Mark your answer on your answer sheet.

18. Mark your answer on your answer sheet.

19. Mark your answer on your answer sheet.

20. Mark your answer on your answer sheet.

21. Mark your answer on your answer sheet.

22. Mark your answer on your answer sheet.

23. Mark your answer on your answer sheet.

24. Mark your answer on your answer sheet.

25. Mark your answer on your answer sheet.

26. Mark your answer on your answer sheet.

27. Mark your answer on your answer sheet.

28. Mark your answer on your answer sheet.

29. Mark your answer on your answer sheet.

30. Mark your answer on your answer sheet.

31. Mark your answer on your answer sheet.

PART 3

Directions: In this part, you will listen to several conversations between two or more speakers. These conversations will not be printed and will only be spoken one time. For each conversation, you will be asked to answer three questions. Select the best response and mark the corresponding letter (A), (B), (C), or (D) on your answer sheet.

32. Where most likely is the conversation taking place?

   (A) At a government office
   (B) At a manufacturing plant
   (C) At an accommodation facility
   (D) At a convention center

33. According to the man, what did the speakers discuss this morning?

   (A) Schedule changes
   (B) Machinery prices
   (C) Building renovations
   (D) Malfunctioning equipment

34. What problem does the woman mention?

   (A) There is not much preparation time.
   (B) An evaluation went poorly.
   (C) There are not enough employees.
   (D) A regulation has been altered.

35. What does the man offer to do?

   (A) Give the woman a menu
   (B) Purchase a beverage
   (C) Make a pot of coffee
   (D) Contact a café manager

36. What does the man mean when he says, "I think that one was discontinued"?

   (A) A seasonal promotion was changed.
   (B) A flavor was unsuccessful.
   (C) Some merchandise will be refunded.
   (D) Some new items have been reordered.

37. Why must a special request be made?

   (A) The woman is in a rush.
   (B) The woman is on a diet.
   (C) The man has a coupon.
   (D) The man has an allergy.

38. What does the man ask the woman to do?

   (A) Scan some documents
   (B) Postpone a departure date
   (C) Come up with an agenda
   (D) Complete some reports

39. Why is the woman going out of town?

   (A) To attend a shareholders' meeting
   (B) To sign a sales contract
   (C) To speak at a team seminar
   (D) To participate in a celebration

40. According to the woman, what is Catherine Dawkins willing to do?

   (A) Switch divisions
   (B) Work additional hours
   (C) Lead an accounting team
   (D) Increase a budget

41. What did the man do two weeks ago?

   (A) Returned a book to a store
   (B) Sent a package overseas
   (C) Bought an item
   (D) Enrolled in a course

42. What does the woman say the man failed to provide?

   (A) A book title
   (B) A recipient name
   (C) An e-mail address
   (D) A unit number

43. What does the woman recommend?

   (A) Talking to a property manager
   (B) Using another courier service
   (C) Correcting some billing information
   (D) Placing an order through a Web site

GO ON TO THE NEXT PAGE

44. What is the conversation mainly about?

    (A) A cell phone plan
    (B) A new product model
    (C) A special promotional offer
    (D) A business's warranty policy

45. What is mentioned about the Verso X3?

    (A) It was recently released.
    (B) It was recalled by the manufacturer.
    (C) It can be ordered online.
    (D) It can be upgraded for free.

46. What will most likely happen next?

    (A) The man will give a demonstration.
    (B) The man will explain some options.
    (C) The woman's profile will be updated.
    (D) The woman's device will be
        examined.

___

47. What is the woman in charge of?

    (A) Hiring new architects
    (B) Correcting an e-mail error
    (C) Planning a meeting
    (D) Gathering some files

48. Why will more time be allowed for Helen?

    (A) She lives far away from a building.
    (B) She has not finished a design.
    (C) She will be showing a visitor around.
    (D) She needs more time for a
        presentation.

49. What will the woman most likely do next?

    (A) Photocopy some printouts
    (B) Revise an agenda
    (C) Reserve a conference room
    (D) Take a lunch break

___

50. How can employees secure time off?

    (A) By completing the necessary form
    (B) By calling the human resources
        department
    (C) By sending an e-mail to a director
    (D) By placing paperwork in a mailbox

51. According to the woman, why might the
    man's request be denied?

    (A) A colleague is not in the office.
    (B) Some teams are understaffed.
    (C) A manager was not notified in
        advance.
    (D) Other people have submitted
        applications.

52. What will the man probably do next?

    (A) Review some instructions
    (B) Share notes with a coworker
    (C) Speak with a supervisor
    (D) Change some travel arrangements

___

53. What are the speakers mainly discussing?

    (A) International travel plans
    (B) Foreign language lessons
    (C) An overseas branch opening
    (D) An educational publication

54. What information does Jenny provide?

    (A) The costs of enrollment
    (B) The number of students
    (C) The start date of a course
    (D) The material list for a class

55. What is the man eligible to receive?

    (A) A special fee reduction
    (B) A free online lecture
    (C) A membership upgrade
    (D) A complimentary handout

___

56. What type of business do the speakers most likely work for?

(A) A television station
(B) An advertising firm
(C) A furniture retailer
(D) A fashion design company

57. What does the man suggest?

(A) Forwarding a staff memo
(B) Passing out some surveys
(C) Promoting outdoor merchandise
(D) Turning in an assignment

58. Why does the man say, "Alyssa's at an off-site training session all day today"?

(A) To express concern about a deadline
(B) To explain why he will work alone
(C) To clarify who will miss an orientation
(D) To ask for help from other team members

---

59. Why does the man call the woman?

(A) To follow up on an agreement
(B) To discuss unpaid charges
(C) To describe service coverage
(D) To encourage an expansion

60. What does the woman say about the legal team?

(A) It has been downsized.
(B) It is checking a document.
(C) It has acquired a license.
(D) It is being evaluated.

61. Why does the man congratulate the woman?

(A) A firm has received an award.
(B) A safety inspection was passed.
(C) A distributor has been contracted.
(D) A product has attracted attention.

Pain Relief Medication	Price Per Box	Price Per Pill
UltraMed	$3.50	10¢
NoAche	$4.50	8¢
HealFast	$5.50	12¢
SootheNow	$7.50	9¢

62. What did the man already do?

(A) Cleared products from the shelves
(B) Contacted a drug manufacturer
(C) Assisted some customers
(D) Reviewed stock levels

63. Why is cough medicine in short supply?

(A) An illness is common at the moment.
(B) A delivery has not arrived on schedule.
(C) A firm has stopped producing goods.
(D) A new brand was recently released.

64. Look at the graphic. Which item will the man order?

(A) UltraMed
(B) NoAche
(C) HealFast
(D) SootheNow

GO ON TO THE NEXT PAGE

Building A			Triton Theater		

Maria Street | Flora Road | Riviera Street

Building A | | Triton Theater
| | Building B | Truro Avenue | | Building C |
| | | Fresco Road | | |
Waverly Park | Building D

65. According to the man, how many art tours does Tuscan Sun Excursions operate daily?

(A) 1
(B) 2
(C) 3
(D) 4

66. Look at the graphic. Where most likely does the woman want to go?

(A) To Building A
(B) To Building B
(C) To Building C
(D) To Building D

67. What does the man offer to do?

(A) Provide contact information
(B) Make some reservations
(C) Get a map of a downtown area
(D) Telephone a local gallery

Nutrition Facts

Serving Size: 10 pretzels
Servings per Pack: 3

Ingredient	Amount per Serving
Sugar	6g
Carbohydrates	32g
Fat	22g
Cholesterol	20mg

68. Where is the conversation most likely taking place?

(A) At a restaurant
(B) At an office building
(C) At a convenience store
(D) At an airport

69. Look at the graphic. Which ingredient amount is too high for the man?

(A) 6g
(B) 32g
(C) 22g
(D) 20mg

70. What does the man say he will do?

(A) Pick another snack
(B) Wait for a meal
(C) Read a product label
(D) Inquire about a lunch menu

PART 4

Directions: In this part, you will listen to several short talks by a single speaker. These talks will not be printed and will only be spoken one time. For each talk, you will be asked to answer three questions. Select the best response and mark the corresponding letter (A), (B), (C), or (D) on your answer sheet.

71. Where most likely are the listeners?
    (A) At a museum
    (B) At an art school
    (C) At a public library
    (D) At a painting studio

72. According to the speaker, what is unusual about *The Flames of Clouds*?
    (A) Its size
    (B) Its use of color
    (C) Its date of origin
    (D) Its name

73. What will listeners most likely do next?
    (A) Read about some artwork
    (B) Visit a gift shop
    (C) Watch a brief video
    (D) Go to another gallery

74. What type of business is being advertised?
    (A) An online retailer
    (B) A catering company
    (C) A food outlet
    (D) A department store

75. According to the speaker, what distinguishes the company from its competitors?
    (A) Reasonable prices
    (B) Unlimited toppings
    (C) Unique flavors
    (D) Natural ingredients

76. Why should listeners visit the business's social media page?
    (A) Some deals are available.
    (B) A newsletter was published.
    (C) A menu can be downloaded.
    (D) Some reviews have been posted.

77. Why is the speaker addressing the audience?
    (A) To apologize for a delay
    (B) To introduce a director
    (C) To announce a change
    (D) To discuss an actor's role

78. What can listeners obtain from a staff member?
    (A) Photos of cast members
    (B) Gift certificates
    (C) Programs for the event
    (D) Complimentary tickets

79. What does the speaker imply when he says, "We received complaints about people eating during our last production"?
    (A) A regulation was no longer followed.
    (B) A problem is difficult to resolve.
    (C) A decision will be made soon.
    (D) A policy was recently altered.

80. What is Dr. Mattson's area of expertise?
    (A) Economics
    (B) Journalism
    (C) Statistics
    (D) Ecology

81. According to the speaker, what was released on Monday?
    (A) An academic publication
    (B) A podcast series
    (C) A policy review
    (D) A list of keynote speakers

82. What is mentioned about Dr. Mattson?
    (A) He will address some criticisms.
    (B) He will take calls from listeners.
    (C) He will talk about a course curriculum.
    (D) He will submit a research proposal.

GO ON TO THE NEXT PAGE

83. Where do the listeners most likely work?

    (A) At an educational institution
    (B) At a cosmetics firm
    (C) At an advertising company
    (D) At an electronics manufacturer

84. Why does the speaker say, "I don't want to turn anyone away, though"?

    (A) She will provide a solution.
    (B) She will reconsider a decision.
    (C) She will approve a plan.
    (D) She will reject a request.

85. What will Beth Meyers most likely do?

    (A) Try out some products
    (B) Organize an activity
    (C) Attend a meeting
    (D) Contact applicants

86. What is Ivan Schwartz's occupation?

    (A) Consultant
    (B) Travel agent
    (C) Programmer
    (D) Instructor

87. According to the speaker, what will Ivan Schwartz do?

    (A) Install some equipment
    (B) Oversee an ongoing project
    (C) Create a computer application
    (D) Learn about new software

88. What are listeners asked to do?

    (A) Undergo some training
    (B) Welcome a colleague
    (C) Set up an office for a manager
    (D) Prepare for a business trip

89. Why does the speaker thank the listener?

    (A) For making a restaurant reservation
    (B) For inviting her to a social gathering
    (C) For supporting a local charity
    (D) For providing her with class information

90. What does the speaker imply when she says, "Could you give me her contact information"?

    (A) She was contacted by a neighbor.
    (B) She wants to apply to a firm.
    (C) She may hire a designer.
    (D) She will reschedule an appointment.

91. What problem is mentioned?

    (A) A course was canceled.
    (B) A fee has been increased.
    (C) A facility will close down.
    (D) A service is no longer offered.

92. What is the purpose of the report?

    (A) To describe promotional efforts
    (B) To discuss an upcoming election
    (C) To explain tour restrictions
    (D) To outline a construction project

93. According to the speaker, what does Shenzhen possess?

    (A) A world-renowned shopping complex
    (B) Favorable tax rates
    (C) An international airport
    (D) Numerous vacant retail spaces

94. What do officials think about Shenzhen?

    (A) It currently has a high population.
    (B) It is experiencing increases in tourism.
    (C) It can achieve further economic success.
    (D) It is a safe place for travelers from abroad.

Subscription Renewal Form

Subscription Period	Fee	Selection
6 months	$30	
12 months	$50	
18 months	$70	√
24 months	$100	

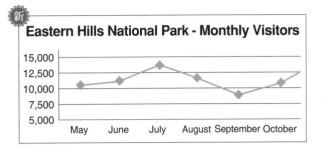

Eastern Hills National Park - Monthly Visitors

95. What does the speaker plan to do in December?

(A) Update her mailing address
(B) Make a subscription payment
(C) Submit a magazine article
(D) Travel overseas for work

96. Look at the graphic. How much does the subscription the speaker is interested in cost?

(A) $30
(B) $50
(C) $70
(D) $100

97. What does the speaker request?

(A) A partial refund
(B) A contract extension
(C) An account closure
(D) An e-mail confirmation

98. How often will buses run beginning next month?

(A) Every 20 minutes
(B) Every 30 minutes
(C) Every 40 minutes
(D) Every 60 minutes

99. Look at the graphic. When will the regular shuttle bus service most likely resume?

(A) In July
(B) In August
(C) In September
(D) In October

100. What is mentioned about Brenda Kirk?

(A) She manages the information center.
(B) She has arranged a lecture series.
(C) She will participate in a training program.
(D) She gave a presentation on the park's history.

解答 p.147 / 分數換算表 p.149 / 題目解析 p.241（解答本）

▌請翻到次頁的「自我檢測表」檢視自己解答問題的方法與態度。
▌請利用 p.147 分數換算表換算完分數。

自我檢測表

順利結束 TEST 06 了嗎？

現在透過以下問題來檢視一下自己的作答情況吧！

1.　我在作答時，中間沒有停下來過。

　　☐ 是　☐ 否

　　若答案為否，理由是為什麼呢？

2.　我有確實劃記答案紙上的每一道題目。

　　☐ 是　☐ 否

　　若答案為否，理由是為什麼呢？

3.　作答 Part 2 的 25 題時，我非常專心於題目上。

　　☐ 是　☐ 否

　　若答案為否，理由是為什麼呢？

4.　作答 Part 3 時，我在聽題目音檔前都已先看過題目和選項。

　　☐ 是　☐ 否

　　若答案為否，理由是為什麼呢？

5.　作答 Part 4 時，我在聽題目音檔前都已先看過題目和選項。

　　☐ 是　☐ 否

　　若答案為否，理由是為什麼呢？

6.　請寫下需要改進之處或給自己的建議。

★請確認自己在進行作答前寫下的目標分數，並再次堅定要達成目標的決心。需要改進的地方務必於下一回測驗中實踐，這一點非常重要，唯有如此才能更進步。

TEST 07

Part 1

Part 2

Part 3 新

Part 4 新

自我評量表

稍等！作答前確認事項：
1. 關掉手機電源了嗎？ □是
2. 準備好答案卡、鉛筆、橡皮擦了嗎？ □是
3. 準備好聽MP3了嗎？ □是

所有準備都完成後，請先預想目標成績，把它寫在後面的自我檢測表上，再開始作答。

TEST 07.mp3 收錄了 Part 1-4。

LISTENING TEST

In this section, you must demonstrate your ability to understand spoken English. This section is divided into four parts and will take approximately 45 minutes to complete. Do not mark the answers in your test book. Use the answer sheet that is provided separately.

PART 1

Directions: For each question, you will listen to four short statements about a picture in your test book. These statements will not be printed and will only be spoken one time. Select the statement that best describes what is happening in the picture and mark the corresponding letter (A), (B), (C), or (D) on the answer sheet.

Sample Answer
Ⓐ ● Ⓒ Ⓓ

The statement that best describes the picture is (B), "The man is sitting at the desk." So, you should mark letter (B) on the answer sheet.

1.

2.

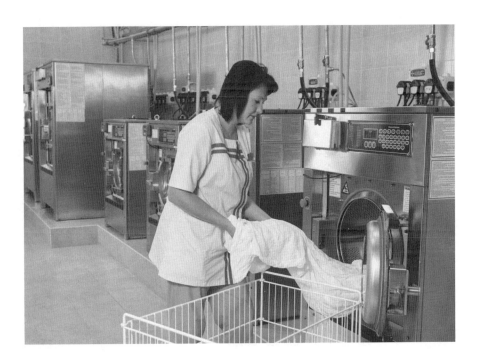

GO ON TO THE NEXT PAGE ➡

3.

4.

5.

6.

GO ON TO THE NEXT PAGE ➔

PART 2

Directions: For each question, you will listen to a statement or question followed by three possible responses spoken in English. They will not be printed and will only be spoken one time. Select the best response and mark the corresponding letter (A), (B), or (C) on your answer sheet.

7. Mark your answer on your answer sheet.

8. Mark your answer on your answer sheet.

9. Mark your answer on your answer sheet.

10. Mark your answer on your answer sheet.

11. Mark your answer on your answer sheet.

12. Mark your answer on your answer sheet.

13. Mark your answer on your answer sheet.

14. Mark your answer on your answer sheet.

15. Mark your answer on your answer sheet.

16. Mark your answer on your answer sheet.

17. Mark your answer on your answer sheet.

18. Mark your answer on your answer sheet.

19. Mark your answer on your answer sheet.

20. Mark your answer on your answer sheet.

21. Mark your answer on your answer sheet.

22. Mark your answer on your answer sheet.

23. Mark your answer on your answer sheet.

24. Mark your answer on your answer sheet.

25. Mark your answer on your answer sheet.

26. Mark your answer on your answer sheet.

27. Mark your answer on your answer sheet.

28. Mark your answer on your answer sheet.

29. Mark your answer on your answer sheet.

30. Mark your answer on your answer sheet.

31. Mark your answer on your answer sheet.

PART 3

Directions: In this part, you will listen to several conversations between two or more speakers. These conversations will not be printed and will only be spoken one time. For each conversation, you will be asked to answer three questions. Select the best response and mark the corresponding letter (A), (B), (C), or (D) on your answer sheet.

32. What task has the woman been assigned?

(A) Planning an event
(B) Revising an annual report
(C) Arranging rides for staff
(D) Promoting a competition

33. What does the man request the woman do?

(A) Lead a team-building exercise
(B) Consider a different date
(C) Speak to a department head
(D) Announce the results of a match

34. What does the man offer to do?

(A) Get passes for a game
(B) Write down some directions
(C) Search for a local business
(D) Message some colleagues

---

35. Who most likely is the man?

(A) A film editor
(B) A television program host
(C) A box office attendant
(D) A movie critic

36. What does the woman ask the man about?

(A) The name of an actor
(B) The availability of a showing
(C) The length of a performance
(D) The price of a ticket

37. What does the man say about Andy Baker?

(A) He will meet with investors.
(B) He attended a cinema opening.
(C) He will respond to some inquiries.
(D) He released a production last year.

38. Where does the man most likely work?

(A) At a travel agency
(B) At a repair shop
(C) At a real estate office
(D) At shopping center

39. What does the man suggest the woman do?

(A) Bring a device to a business
(B) Restart a machine
(C) Install some software
(D) Replace a laptop component

40. What does the man mean when he says, "let me transfer you to Robert now"?

(A) He has to get approval from a superior.
(B) He is unfamiliar with a product model.
(C) He has to leave for a workshop.
(D) He is unable to set up an appointment.

---

41. What are the speakers mainly discussing?

(A) A coworker's vacation
(B) A corporate regulation
(C) An overseas investment
(D) A supervisor's promotion

42. What does the woman ask the man about?

(A) The reason for a change
(B) The duration of a trip
(C) The cost of a renovation
(D) The size of a warehouse

43. What did the woman do last week?

(A) Talked with a manager
(B) Applied for a transfer
(C) Edited a policy manual
(D) Submitted a written complaint

GO ON TO THE NEXT PAGE

44. Where does the conversation probably take place?

(A) At a department store
(B) At a library
(C) At an accounting office
(D) At a bookstore

45. What suggestion does the man make?

(A) Contacting an organization again
(B) Borrowing a specific book
(C) Going to another area
(D) Ordering a replacement card

46. What information does the man need?

(A) An account holder's name
(B) A publication title
(C) An e-mail address
(D) An identification number

47. Why did the man call the woman?

(A) To provide payment details
(B) To reserve some merchandise
(C) To inquire about a piece of gear
(D) To learn about an upcoming launch

48. What does the woman mention about racquet grips?

(A) They are currently out of stock.
(B) They are made with quality materials.
(C) They come in various types.
(D) They have been used by sports stars.

49. What will the man probably do this afternoon?

(A) Attend a tennis class
(B) Browse some items
(C) Call a sales associate
(D) Return some racquets

50. What problem does the woman describe?

(A) She visited the incorrect office.
(B) She lost a financial document.
(C) She does not have a day planner.
(D) She is late for a consultation.

51. What does the woman allow the man to do?

(A) Participate in a conference call
(B) Remove equipment from an office
(C) Send notes to an advisor
(D) Review her personal belongings

52. What detail does the man provide?

(A) A meeting location
(B) A reservation time
(C) A client's name
(D) A coworker's address

53. Where is the conversation most likely taking place?

(A) In a grocery store
(B) In a private residence
(C) In a television studio
(D) In a dining establishment

54. Why does the man say, "you're familiar with this dish"?

(A) To accept a recommendation about a recipe
(B) To show appreciation for a cooking tip
(C) To request assistance with a demonstration
(D) To express agreement regarding an ingredient

55. What will the man most likely do next?

(A) Explain food differences
(B) Read over menu options
(C) Consult with a culinary expert
(D) Put away some utensils

56. What department does the man work in?

(A) Administration
(B) Marketing
(C) Finance
(D) Research

57. What does the man imply when he says, "I requested a deadline extension"?

(A) He will reschedule a business meeting.
(B) He will deal with other problems.
(C) He will appear at a gathering.
(D) He will expand a work project.

58. What does the woman offer to do?

(A) Give some notes to a superior
(B) Sign a colleague up for an event
(C) Make a personal donation
(D) Revise some reports

59. What does the team leader want the man to do?

(A) Hire a branch manager
(B) Give an award to a top performer
(C) Present some diagrams
(D) Choose a representative

60. Why is the man worried?

(A) A process may take too long.
(B) A presentation did not go well.
(C) A chart has been misplaced.
(D) An audit is approaching.

61. What does the man ask the woman to do?

(A) Update a mailing list
(B) Turn in an application
(C) Share a template
(D) Meet with a designer

62. Where most likely do the speakers work?

(A) At an advertising company
(B) At an educational institution
(C) At an engineering firm
(D) At a staffing agency

63. What is implied about South Bend Corporation?

(A) It is unsatisfied with a candidate.
(B) It wants to negotiate some prices.
(C) It terminated some employees.
(D) It hired a business in the past.

64. How long will the speakers have to complete a task?

(A) Three weeks
(B) Four weeks
(C) Five weeks
(D) Six weeks

GO ON TO THE NEXT PAGE

Oceans Alive

Buy one, get one free
(Good for all organic merchandise)
Sold at SuperSmart
Valid until March 31

65. What problem does the woman mention?

(A) A manager is not available.
(B) A soap line received poor reviews.
(C) A team is understaffed.
(D) An assignment has not been finished.

66. What kind of event will be held next month?

(A) A product release
(B) A trade show
(C) A yearly sale
(D) An awards ceremony

67. Look at the graphic. Which product is not covered by the coupon?

(A) Shampoo
(B) Hand soap
(C) Face cleanser
(D) Body wash

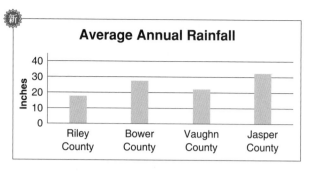

68. What does the man ask the woman about?

(A) Why an analysis was performed
(B) When construction will begin
(C) Whether an assessment is finished
(D) If an amusement park has opened

69. What was the woman responsible for?

(A) Conducting an examination
(B) Selecting a meeting place
(C) Printing a map of a region
(D) Securing a business contract

70. Look at the graphic. Which county has been recommended?

(A) Riley County
(B) Bower County
(C) Vaughn County
(D) Jasper County

PART 4

Directions: In this part, you will listen to several short talks by a single speaker. These talks will not be printed and will only be spoken one time. For each talk, you will be asked to answer three questions. Select the best response and mark the corresponding letter (A), (B), (C), or (D) on your answer sheet.

71. Where does the listener probably work?

  (A) At a travel agency
  (B) At a media company
  (C) At a financial firm
  (D) At a law office

72. What will the speaker do on Monday?

  (A) Prepare a report
  (B) Go to the airport
  (C) Attend a convention
  (D) Give a presentation

73. What information does the speaker ask for?

  (A) Restaurant recommendations
  (B) Clients' names
  (C) A meeting agenda
  (D) An order number

74. At what event is the speech being given?

  (A) A service center opening
  (B) A product launch party
  (C) A monthly shareholders meeting
  (D) A company anniversary celebration

75. Why does the speaker praise Patricia Sanderson?

  (A) She altered a logo design.
  (B) She designed a popular Web site.
  (C) She suggested a device feature.
  (D) She signed an important client.

76. What will most likely happen next?

  (A) An employee will be introduced.
  (B) A device will be demonstrated.
  (C) A speech will be given.
  (D) A video will be played.

77. What did the listener do on Thursday?

  (A) Submitted an application
  (B) E-mailed a manager
  (C) Participated in an interview
  (D) Revised a contract

78. What was the CEO impressed with?

  (A) A proposal to boost sales
  (B) A plan to train new employees
  (C) A design for a home appliance
  (D) A suggestion for a brochure

79. What does the speaker mean when she says, "the current manager will be retiring in three weeks"?

  (A) A schedule will likely be updated.
  (B) A decision must be made quickly.
  (C) An employee will be promoted soon.
  (D) A position has just become available.

80. Where most likely are the listeners?

  (A) At a construction site
  (B) At a medical clinic
  (C) At a manufacturing plant
  (D) At a car dealership

81. According to the speaker, what has been changed?

  (A) The price of some merchandise
  (B) The order of a tour
  (C) The type of machines used
  (D) The operational hours of a facility

82. What are listeners instructed to do?

  (A) Avoid touching equipment
  (B) Read an instruction manual
  (C) Wear protective gear
  (D) Enroll in a class

GO ON TO THE NEXT PAGE

83. What is the message mainly about?

(A) A new menu
(B) A recent critique
(C) A facility reopening
(D) A catering inquiry

84. Why does the speaker say, "Ms. Clay has very high standards"?

(A) To indicate regret
(B) To express anticipation
(C) To explain a recurring request
(D) To complain about a coworker

85. What does the speaker ask the listener to do?

(A) Adjust a recipe
(B) Organize a party
(C) Post a review online
(D) Visit a newspaper office

---

86. What is the advertisement mainly about?

(A) A radio program
(B) An awards ceremony
(C) An acting audition
(D) A musical contest

87. What does the speaker say about the judges?

(A) They will be former contestants.
(B) They will choose the final winner.
(C) They will be changed each week.
(D) They will consider viewer feedback.

88. What does the speaker say is available on the Web site?

(A) An audio recording
(B) A venue list
(C) A performance schedule
(D) A film trailer

---

89. What is mentioned about the previous speakers?

(A) They worked for major publications.
(B) They graduated from James College.
(C) They gave stimulating lectures.
(D) They received writing prizes.

90. What will the speaker talk about?

(A) The importance of reading
(B) The influence of literature
(C) The value of higher education
(D) The effects of legal reform

91. Who is Jack Coyle?

(A) An author
(B) A college lecturer
(C) A public official
(D) A lawyer

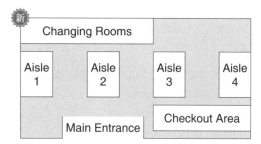

92. Who is the speaker most likely addressing?

(A) Store customers
(B) Marketing consultants
(C) Shop employees
(D) Construction workers

93. Look at the graphic. Where has the display been set up?

(A) In Aisle 1
(B) In Aisle 2
(C) In Aisle 3
(D) In Aisle 4

94. According to the speaker, what will be announced tomorrow?

(A) The dates of a renovation project
(B) The name of a design firm
(C) The details of a sportswear production
(D) The location of a new branch

Monthly Sales

	July	August	September
$35,000			
$30,000			▓
$25,000	▓	▓	
$20,000			
$15,000			
$10,000			

95. What did the speaker do yesterday?

(A) Visited a business
(B) Looked at some data
(C) Went to a sales conference
(D) Gave a presentation

96. Look at the graphic. Which branch does the graph refer to?

(A) Kingston
(B) Albany
(C) Bethany
(D) Newark

97. What will most likely happen next?

(A) A report will be revised.
(B) A manager will be introduced.
(C) A document will be distributed.
(D) A store will be contacted.

STEP 1	Meet with clients
STEP 2	Discuss plan with team leader
STEP 3	Draft blueprints
STEP 4	Modify plans based on feedback
STEP 5	Submit for approval

98. What happened last month?

(A) A permit application was rejected.
(B) A structure was inspected.
(C) A project was started.
(D) A sports arena was completed.

99. Why is a change being made?

(A) To reduce some expenses
(B) To reflect client requests
(C) To improve communication
(D) To accommodate time constraints

100. Look at the graphic. Which step was removed from a work process?

(A) Meet with clients
(B) Discuss plan with team leader
(C) Modify plans based on feedback
(D) Submit for approval

LISTENING

1 2 3 4 5 6 7 8 9 10

解答 **p.147** / 分數換算表 **p.149** / 題目解析 **p.285**（解答本）

▌請翻到次頁的「自我檢測表」檢視自己解答問題的方法與態度。
▌請利用 **p.147** 分數換算表換算完分數。

自我檢測表

順利結束 TEST 07 了嗎？

現在透過以下問題來檢視一下自己的作答情況吧！

1.　我在作答時，中間沒有停下來過。

　　☐ 是　☐ 否

　　若答案為否，理由是為什麼呢？

2.　我有確實劃記答案紙上的每一道題目。

　　☐ 是　☐ 否

　　若答案為否，理由是為什麼呢？

3.　作答 Part 2 的 25 題時，我非常專心於題目上。

　　☐ 是　☐ 否

　　若答案為否，理由是為什麼呢？

4.　作答 Part 3 時，我在聽題目音檔前都已先看過題目和選項。

　　☐ 是　☐ 否

　　若答案為否，理由是為什麼呢？

5.　作答 Part 4 時，我在聽題目音檔前都已先看過題目和選項。

　　☐ 是　☐ 否

　　若答案為否，理由是為什麼呢？

6.　請寫下需要改進之處或給自己的建議。

★請確認自己在進行作答前寫下的目標分數，並再次堅定要達成目標的決心。需要改進的地方務必
　於下一回測驗中實踐，這一點非常重要，唯有如此才能更進步。

TEST 08

Part 1

Part 2

Part 3 新

Part 4 新

自我評量表

稍等！作答前確認事項：
1. 關掉手機電源了嗎？ □是
2. 準備好答案卡、鉛筆、橡皮擦了嗎？ □是
3. 準備好聽MP3了嗎？ □是

所有準備都完成後，請先預想目標成績，把它寫在後面的自我檢測表上，再開始作答。

TEST 08.mp3 收錄了 Part 1-4。

LISTENING TEST

In this section, you must demonstrate your ability to understand spoken English. This section is divided into four parts and will take approximately 45 minutes to complete. Do not mark the answers in your test book. Use the answer sheet that is provided separately.

PART 1

Directions: For each question, you will listen to four short statements about a picture in your test book. These statements will not be printed and will only be spoken one time. Select the statement that best describes what is happening in the picture and mark the corresponding letter (A), (B), (C), or (D) on the answer sheet.

Sample Answer
Ⓐ ● Ⓒ Ⓓ

The statement that best describes the picture is (B), "The man is sitting at the desk." So, you should mark letter (B) on the answer sheet.

1.

2.

GO ON TO THE NEXT PAGE

3.

4.

5.

6.

GO ON TO THE NEXT PAGE

PART 2

Directions: For each question, you will listen to a statement or question followed by three possible responses spoken in English. They will not be printed and will only be spoken one time. Select the best response and mark the corresponding letter (A), (B), or (C) on your answer sheet.

7. Mark your answer on your answer sheet.

8. Mark your answer on your answer sheet.

9. Mark your answer on your answer sheet.

10. Mark your answer on your answer sheet.

11. Mark your answer on your answer sheet.

12. Mark your answer on your answer sheet.

13. Mark your answer on your answer sheet.

14. Mark your answer on your answer sheet.

15. Mark your answer on your answer sheet.

16. Mark your answer on your answer sheet.

17. Mark your answer on your answer sheet.

18. Mark your answer on your answer sheet.

19. Mark your answer on your answer sheet.

20. Mark your answer on your answer sheet.

21. Mark your answer on your answer sheet.

22. Mark your answer on your answer sheet.

23. Mark your answer on your answer sheet.

24. Mark your answer on your answer sheet.

25. Mark your answer on your answer sheet.

26. Mark your answer on your answer sheet.

27. Mark your answer on your answer sheet.

28. Mark your answer on your answer sheet.

29. Mark your answer on your answer sheet.

30. Mark your answer on your answer sheet.

31. Mark your answer on your answer sheet.

PART 3

Directions: In this part, you will listen to several conversations between two or more speakers. These conversations will not be printed and will only be spoken one time. For each conversation, you will be asked to answer three questions. Select the best response and mark the corresponding letter (A), (B), (C), or (D) on your answer sheet.

32. Who most likely are the speakers?

(A) Park rangers
(B) Construction workers
(C) Florists
(D) Landscapers

33. What does the man want to do first?

(A) Prepare the ground for plants
(B) Fill in holes with dirt
(C) Go on an early lunch break
(D) Clean out the back of a truck

34. What problem does the man mention?

(A) A cart was left behind.
(B) A bush cannot be removed.
(C) A glove was damaged.
(D) A shovel is not large enough.

35. What is the woman trying to find?

(A) A spray cleaner
(B) A power drill
(C) Some artwork
(D) Some hooks

36. Why does the woman reject an offer?

(A) She is being assisted by other staff.
(B) She is not interested in a promotion.
(C) She knows where some items are stocked.
(D) She knows why a product is sold out.

37. According to the man, how can the woman get more information?

(A) By downloading an application
(B) By picking up a shop directory
(C) By seeking out employees
(D) By using a device

38. Where does the conversation take place?

(A) At a company gym
(B) At a sports arena
(C) At a luxury resort
(D) At an architectural studio

39. What is the purpose of the man's visit?

(A) To view changes to a facility
(B) To watch an athletic event
(C) To recommend building improvements
(D) To submit blueprints for a structure

40. What does the woman say about VIP guests?

(A) They can receive a price reduction.
(B) They are waiting in a seating area.
(C) They are pleased with the modifications.
(D) They will have access to a special section.

41. What problem does the man mention?

(A) A list has been misplaced.
(B) A software program has errors.
(C) A conference has been postponed.
(D) A department member is late.

42. What does the woman suggest?

(A) Registering for a workshop
(B) Speaking with a technician
(C) Using a database
(D) Taking some notes

43. Why does the man say, "I was in Richmond"?

(A) To apologize for a mistake
(B) To clarify a decision
(C) To explain his absence
(D) To describe his vacation

GO ON TO THE NEXT PAGE

44. Who most likely is the woman?

(A) A repairperson
(B) A salesperson
(C) A janitor
(D) A maintenance worker

45. According to the woman, what is a feature of the product?

(A) It can move itself.
(B) It can be cleaned easily.
(C) It is environmentally friendly.
(D) It comes in various sizes.

46. What will most likely happen next?

(A) A floor will be blocked off.
(B) A store will be restocked.
(C) A device will be used.
(D) An item will be put on sale.

47. What is the problem?

(A) A lobby is crowded.
(B) A drink has been spilled.
(C) A hotel has no vacancies.
(D) A room is too small.

48. What solution does the woman suggest?

(A) Talking to a personnel member
(B) Canceling hotel reservations
(C) Finding some other chairs
(D) Modifying an itinerary

49. Why will the woman be unable to use the swimming pool?

(A) A check-in process was delayed.
(B) A performance has been scheduled.
(C) The facility is being remodeled.
(D) The water is being tested.

50. According to the man, why does the woman require some information?

(A) To prepare a notification
(B) To propose an idea to a supervisor
(C) To respond to client inquiries
(D) To complete a questionnaire

51. What does the man say riders can do online?

(A) Sign up for a newsletter
(B) Request fare reductions
(C) Read about subway routes
(D) Add money to a card

52. What did the woman forget about?

(A) A new fee
(B) A special giveaway
(C) A temporary closure
(D) A station remodel

53. What is mentioned about Mr. Marquez?

(A) He requested a transfer.
(B) He moved to a new position.
(C) He hired a consultant.
(D) He organized a staff activity.

54. What will most likely happen on November third?

(A) Some invitations will be mailed out.
(B) Some employees will listen to a lecture.
(C) A safety procedure will be implemented.
(D) A director will announce a fundraiser date.

55. What is the man concerned about?

(A) A failed inspection
(B) A frequent complaint
(C) A scheduling conflict
(D) An unsuccessful workshop

56. What is the woman planning to do next week?

(A) Entertain some visitors
(B) Book a table at a restaurant
(C) Organize a tour of a factory
(D) Travel to Japan for work

57. What does the man recommend the woman do?

(A) Ask about a down payment
(B) Contact an agent in advance
(C) Place a meal order
(D) Arrange for a boat ride

58. What does the man mention about some local businesses?

(A) They specialize in cruise packages.
(B) They offer reasonably priced rentals.
(C) They will send some representatives.
(D) They will provide area guidebooks.

---

59. Why is the woman calling?

(A) To alert a colleague of a mistake
(B) To notify the man of a problem
(C) To inform a tenant of a policy change
(D) To tell the man about an accident

60. What does the woman want the man to do?

(A) Return a signed document
(B) Remove a waste container
(C) Relocate a vehicle
(D) Clean an apartment unit

61. Why does the man say, "I'll be at work until 5 P.M."?

(A) He is planning to end his shift early.
(B) He is able to attend a session.
(C) He can meet a deadline.
(D) He cannot carry out a task immediately.

Service	Discount	Sale Month
Facial	20% off	March
Haircut	25% off	March
Nail Art	15% off	April
Hair Dyeing	10% off	April

62. What did the woman do last month?

(A) Stopped by an expo center
(B) Bought a hair product
(C) Applied for a salon membership
(D) Made an appointment

63. Look at the graphic. What discount will the woman most likely receive today?

(A) 20 percent off
(B) 25 percent off
(C) 15 percent off
(D) 10 percent off

64. According to the man, what will happen on April 20?

(A) An exhibition will be held.
(B) A new service will be offered.
(C) A discount amount will be increased.
(D) A beauty treatment will be introduced.

GO ON TO THE NEXT PAGE

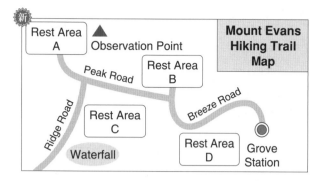

65. What does the woman offer to do?

   (A) Borrow some hiking gear
   (B) Take pictures of a landscape
   (C) Purchase some refreshments
   (D) Contact a station official

66. According to the woman, what happened last week?

   (A) A path was officially opened.
   (B) A picnic area was used for an event.
   (C) A hike had to be postponed.
   (D) A storm created poor conditions.

67. Look at the graphic. Where does the woman suggest taking a break?

   (A) At Rest Area A
   (B) At Rest Area B
   (C) At Rest Area C
   (D) At Rest Area D

From	Subject	Date
Ken Powers	Thanks for Your Order	August 6
Ken Powers	RE: Complaint about Order #4991	August 12
Raymond Liu	RE: Coupon Specifications	August 13
Linda Wright	Question about Taxi Cost	August 15

68. What does the man imply about the jackets?

   (A) They will be featured in a publication.
   (B) They will be kept at an art studio.
   (C) They were paid for with a gift card.
   (D) They were imported from overseas.

69. Look at the graphic. When did the woman receive a discount coupon?

   (A) On August 6
   (B) On August 12
   (C) On August 13
   (D) On August 15

70. According to the woman, what happened earlier today?

   (A) A consultation with a photographer
   (B) A launch for a clothing line
   (C) A show for fashion designers
   (D) A gathering with the media

PART 4

Directions: In this part, you will listen to several short talks by a single speaker. These talks will not be printed and will only be spoken one time. For each talk, you will be asked to answer three questions. Select the best response and mark the corresponding letter (A), (B), (C), or (D) on your answer sheet.

71. Why is the speaker calling?

(A) To request a payment
(B) To answer a question
(C) To ask for additional shirts
(D) To report a problem

72. What will most likely happen on Friday?

(A) An order will be sent.
(B) Staff members will receive training.
(C) A project will get underway.
(D) T-shirt designs will be changed.

73. What does the speaker offer to do?

(A) Contact a designer
(B) Exchange a product
(C) Reduce a charge
(D) Provide a work sample

74. Where do the listeners most likely work?

(A) At a research facility
(B) At a medical clinic
(C) At a service center
(D) At a staffing agency

75. Why does the speaker say, "we don't know who has an appointment tomorrow"?

(A) To complain about an event program
(B) To indicate the need for more staff
(C) To emphasize the urgency of a task
(D) To address a recent question

76. What does the speaker mention about Janet Lee?

(A) She is currently on leave.
(B) She has contacted some customers.
(C) She will distribute a document.
(D) She was recently promoted.

77. Who most likely is the speaker?

(A) An accountant
(B) A researcher
(C) A lawyer
(D) A realtor

78. What does the speaker imply when she says, "few people have shown interest"?

(A) A request cannot be granted.
(B) A deadline may be extended.
(C) A fee cannot be reduced.
(D) A contract may be revised.

79. When will the listener most likely meet Mr. Patterson?

(A) On Thursday
(B) On Friday
(C) On Saturday
(D) On Sunday

80. According to the speaker, what type of event did the CEO arrange?

(A) An industry convention
(B) A company orientation
(C) A fund-raising dinner
(D) A corporate retreat

81. What are listeners expected to do over the next few days?

(A) Watch some instructional videos
(B) Participate in group activities
(C) Discuss potential trip destinations
(D) Share updates with a board member

82. Why must listeners meet at 4 P.M.?

(A) To pose for a photograph
(B) To take a tour of a resort
(C) To make decisions about an event
(D) To listen to a talk from an executive

GO ON TO THE NEXT PAGE

83. What sector does the speaker represent?

    (A) Emergency services
    (B) Transportation
    (C) Education
    (D) Health care

84. What is scheduled to take place next month?

    (A) A training workshop
    (B) A career information session
    (C) A building safety inspection
    (D) A student performance

85. According to the speaker, what would a representative need to do?

    (A) Describe the nature of a position
    (B) Explain the flaws in some gear
    (C) Provide advice on public speaking
    (D) Show participants around a facility

---

86. What did the city council do?

    (A) Voted to change a tax code
    (B) Updated an outdated policy
    (C) Decided to demolish a building
    (D) Held a debate on safety standards

87. Who is John Hamilton?

    (A) A government official
    (B) A historian
    (C) An architect
    (D) A park employee

88. What will happen on Friday?

    (A) A plan will be announced.
    (B) An inspection will take place.
    (C) A meeting will be held.
    (D) A facility will open.

---

89. What task have the listeners been assigned?

    (A) Developing an event for local tourists
    (B) Determining how to target foreign visitors
    (C) Creating a new attraction
    (D) Planning an international fund-raiser

90. What does the speaker say about the snow sculptures?

    (A) They are at risk of melting.
    (B) They take a long time to construct.
    (C) They are popular among attendees.
    (D) They were previously featured in flyers.

91. What will the listeners do in 30 minutes?

    (A) Take a break
    (B) Listen to a speech
    (C) Watch a presentation
    (D) Discuss some ideas

---

92. Who most likely are the listeners?

    (A) Personnel managers
    (B) Sales representatives
    (C) Administrative assistants
    (D) Customer service agents

93. What will most likely happen next?

    (A) A demonstration will be given.
    (B) A manual will be handed out.
    (C) Job duties will be explained.
    (D) Evaluations will be conducted.

94. Why does the speaker say, "You may be surprised by the results"?

    (A) To suggest that a product is popular
    (B) To point out the disadvantages of a plan
    (C) To indicate that a method is effective
    (D) To show the accuracy of some data

Broadcast Schedule	
Wednesday Afternoons (April)	
12:00-2:00	*Health Check*
2:00-2:20	Traffic Report
2:20-3:30	*Culture Break*
3:30-5:00	*Investment Strategies*
5:00-5:10	Weather Update
5:10-6:00	*Gourmet Cooking*

EZ Auto Rentals

Customer: Janis Lyle

Rental Period: October 12-19

Branch: Manchester, England

Receipt #: 84758

Vehicle Rental:	£125.00
Fuel:	£45.00
Collision Insurance:	£75.00
Navigation System:	£25.00
Total:	£270.00

95. What does the speaker mention about Jeff Wallace?

  (A) He has hosted other radio programs.
  (B) He travels often for his job.
  (C) He was the owner of a company.
  (D) He is planning to retire soon.

96. According to the speaker, what might some callers receive?

  (A) A bus pass
  (B) A hotel voucher
  (C) An airline ticket
  (D) A guidebook

97. Look at the graphic. Which show will be replaced?

  (A) *Health Check*
  (B) *Culture Break*
  (C) *Investment Strategies*
  (D) *Gourmet Cooking*

98. What did the speaker do last week?

  (A) Visited some relatives
  (B) Met with a customer
  (C) Attended a convention
  (D) Toured an overseas branch

99. Look at the graphic. How much will the woman be refunded?

  (A) £125.00
  (B) £45.00
  (C) £75.00
  (D) £25.00

100. What does the speaker request be sent to her?

  (A) Promotional materials
  (B) A customer satisfaction survey
  (C) Insurance documents
  (D) An updated invoice

LISTENING 1 2 3 4 5 6 7 8 9 10

解答 p.147 / 分數換算表 p.149 / 題目解析 p.329（解答本）

▌請翻到次頁的「自我檢測表」檢視自己解答問題的方法與態度。
▌請利用 p.147 分數換算表換算完分數。

自我檢測表

順利結束 TEST 08 了嗎？

現在透過以下問題來檢視一下自己的作答情況吧！

1. 我在作答時，中間沒有停下來過。

   □ 是　□ 否

   若答案為否，理由是為什麼呢？

2. 我有確實劃記答案紙上的每一道題目。

   □ 是　□ 否

   若答案為否，理由是為什麼呢？

3. 作答 Part 2 的 25 題時，我非常專心於題目上。

   □ 是　□ 否

   若答案為否，理由是為什麼呢？

4. 作答 Part 3 時，我在聽題目音檔前都已先看過題目和選項。

   □ 是　□ 否

   若答案為否，理由是為什麼呢？

5. 作答 Part 4 時，我在聽題目音檔前都已先看過題目和選項。

   □ 是　□ 否

   若答案為否，理由是為什麼呢？

6. 請寫下需要改進之處或給自己的建議。

★請確認自己在進行作答前寫下的目標分數，並再次堅定要達成目標的決心。需要改進的地方務必
　於下一回測驗中實踐，這一點非常重要，唯有如此才能更進步。

TEST 09

Part 1

Part 2

Part 3 新

Part 4 新

自我評量表

稍等！作答前確認事項：
1. 關掉手機電源了嗎？ □是
2. 準備好答案卡、鉛筆、橡皮擦了嗎？ □是
3. 準備好聽MP3了嗎？ □是

所有準備都完成後，請先預想目標成績，把它寫在後面的自我檢測表上，再開始作答。

🎧 **TEST 09.mp3 收錄了 Part 1-4。**

LISTENING TEST

In this section, you must demonstrate your ability to understand spoken English. This section is divided into four parts and will take approximately 45 minutes to complete. Do not mark the answers in your test book. Use the answer sheet that is provided separately.

PART 1

Directions: For each question, you will listen to four short statements about a picture in your test book. These statements will not be printed and will only be spoken one time. Select the statement that best describes what is happening in the picture and mark the corresponding letter (A), (B), (C), or (D) on the answer sheet.

Sample Answer
Ⓐ ● Ⓒ Ⓓ

The statement that best describes the picture is (B), "The man is sitting at the desk." So, you should mark letter (B) on the answer sheet.

1.

2.

GO ON TO THE NEXT PAGE ➡

3.

4.

5.

6.

GO ON TO THE NEXT PAGE

PART 2

Directions: For each question, you will listen to a statement or question followed by three possible responses spoken in English. They will not be printed and will only be spoken one time. Select the best response and mark the corresponding letter (A), (B), or (C) on your answer sheet.

7. Mark your answer on your answer sheet.

8. Mark your answer on your answer sheet.

9. Mark your answer on your answer sheet.

10. Mark your answer on your answer sheet.

11. Mark your answer on your answer sheet.

12. Mark your answer on your answer sheet.

13. Mark your answer on your answer sheet.

14. Mark your answer on your answer sheet.

15. Mark your answer on your answer sheet.

16. Mark your answer on your answer sheet.

17. Mark your answer on your answer sheet.

18. Mark your answer on your answer sheet.

19. Mark your answer on your answer sheet.

20. Mark your answer on your answer sheet.

21. Mark your answer on your answer sheet.

22. Mark your answer on your answer sheet.

23. Mark your answer on your answer sheet.

24. Mark your answer on your answer sheet.

25. Mark your answer on your answer sheet.

26. Mark your answer on your answer sheet.

27. Mark your answer on your answer sheet.

28. Mark your answer on your answer sheet.

29. Mark your answer on your answer sheet.

30. Mark your answer on your answer sheet.

31. Mark your answer on your answer sheet.

PART 3

Directions: In this part, you will listen to several conversations between two or more speakers. These conversations will not be printed and will only be spoken one time. For each conversation, you will be asked to answer three questions. Select the best response and mark the corresponding letter (A), (B), (C), or (D) on your answer sheet.

32. Why is Malinda unable to stay until 5 P.M.?

(A) She is not feeling very well.
(B) She must get a family member.
(C) She has to drop off some supplies.
(D) She will go to a school function.

33. What does the man agree to do?

(A) Call a receptionist
(B) Interview an applicant
(C) Show people around a gym
(D) Fill in for a colleague

34. According to the woman, where did the man previously work?

(A) At a fitness center
(B) At an advertising firm
(C) At a construction company
(D) At a recruitment agency

35. Where do the speakers most likely work?

(A) At a concert hall
(B) At a clothing retail outlet
(C) At a record store
(D) At an electronics repair shop

36. What does the man recommend?

(A) Selling merchandise online
(B) Contacting local performers
(C) Organizing jazz concerts
(D) Giving away prizes

37. According to the woman, what do some customers want?

(A) Artists' signatures
(B) Musical instruments
(C) Limited edition posters
(D) New albums

38. Where most likely does the conversation take place?

(A) At a bus terminal
(B) At a park
(C) At a garage
(D) At a car dealership

39. What does the woman say about her husband?

(A) He forgot to print a document.
(B) He wants to buy a monthly pass.
(C) He is employed by a nearby business.
(D) He is running some errands.

40. What should the woman do when she leaves?

(A) Make a payment
(B) Speak with an attendant
(C) Ask for a ticket
(D) Confirm an appointment

41. When is the man planning to return from Seattle?

(A) On Tuesday
(B) On Wednesday
(C) On Thursday
(D) On Friday

42. What will probably take place tomorrow morning?

(A) A product demonstration
(B) A sales workshop
(C) A marketing presentation
(D) A shareholders' meeting

43. Why does the man say, "I'll take a later flight, then"?

(A) To accept an upgrade
(B) To turn down a proposal
(C) To confirm a departure time
(D) To agree to a request

GO ON TO THE NEXT PAGE

44. What is the conversation mainly about?

(A) Hiring a personal chef
(B) Postponing a luncheon
(C) Eating at an on-site facility
(D) Extending a break period

45. According to the woman, why has there been a change?

(A) To respond to worker comments
(B) To improve safety measures
(C) To reduce company expenses
(D) To accommodate staff schedules

46. When will the man most likely join the woman?

(A) When a restaurant opens
(B) When a work trip ends
(C) When a menu is changed
(D) When a task is completed

---

47. Where most likely do the speakers work?

(A) At a financial firm
(B) At a print shop
(C) At a research institute
(D) At an appliance manufacturer

48. What does the man ask the woman about?

(A) A team's research results
(B) A document's size specifications
(C) An order's delivery date
(D) An assignment's deadline

49. What does the man mean when he says, "It will be easier for me to refer to that"?

(A) He wants to use updated software.
(B) He would rather print a brochure.
(C) He wants to view an electronic file.
(D) He would like to reference a memo.

---

50. Why is the man calling?

(A) To reserve an item
(B) To cancel an account
(C) To request an extension
(D) To make a complaint

51. According to the woman, what did the library do last month?

(A) Launched a Web site
(B) Changed a notification procedure
(C) Increased fines for overdue materials
(D) Ordered new books

52. What does the woman say she can do?

(A) Return a book
(B) Pass on a message
(C) Send an e-mail
(D) Waive a charge

---

53. What was held on Monday?

(A) An employee orientation
(B) A job interview
(C) A staff meeting
(D) A training session

54. What is mentioned about Sheryl Johnson?

(A) She lacks relevant experience.
(B) She will provide a work sample.
(C) She has requested a transfer.
(D) She will lead a seminar.

55. What will the woman probably do next?

(A) Visit another company
(B) Contact an applicant
(C) Discuss a matter with a superior
(D) Place résumés in a filing cabinet

---

56. What is the problem?

    (A) A gathering was noisy.
    (B) An alarm failed to go off.
    (C) A heating system malfunctioned.
    (D) A piece of furniture is uncomfortable.

57. What does the woman imply when she says, "Are you serious"?

    (A) She missed an appointment.
    (B) She has plans for a holiday.
    (C) She is frustrated by a closure.
    (D) She is disappointed with a unit.

58. What does the woman ask the man about?

    (A) The number of an apartment
    (B) The length of a holiday
    (C) The location of some stationery
    (D) The address of a landlord

59. Who most likely is the man?

    (A) A craftsman
    (B) A personal assistant
    (C) A salesperson
    (D) A fashion designer

60. What problem does the woman mention?

    (A) An order arrived late.
    (B) A stock room is messy.
    (C) A price tag is incorrect.
    (D) A product is damaged.

61. What does the woman ask the man to do?

    (A) Supply a receipt
    (B) Wrap a purchase
    (C) Repair an item
    (D) Provide a discount

62. Where is the conversation most likely taking place?

    (A) At a performance venue
    (B) At an amusement park
    (C) At a science museum
    (D) At a shopping mall

63. According to Amy, how long has the facility been in operation?

    (A) For one month
    (B) For two months
    (C) For one year
    (D) For two years

64. Why was the man unaware of an event?

    (A) He is not on a mailing list.
    (B) He could not attend a conference.
    (C) He did not notice a schedule.
    (D) He was given inaccurate information.

GO ON TO THE NEXT PAGE

Employee Name	Extension Number
Monica Pearce	9087
Josh Han	1099
Valarie Dupree	4419
Will Garcia	7893

Eastville Food Festival

Saturday, Aug 20 – Sunday, Aug 21
11 A.M. – 8 P.M.

One-Day Pass Valid for Aug 20
World Culinary Organization Member

65. What will the man do tonight?

(A) Upgrade computer software
(B) Assist with a move
(C) Get in touch with a client
(D) Participate in a meeting

66. What problem does the man mention?

(A) A goal was missed.
(B) A list is incomplete.
(C) A directory is inaccessible.
(D) A desk can no longer be used.

67. Look at the graphic. Who works in the marketing department?

(A) Monica Pearce
(B) Josh Han
(C) Valarie Dupree
(D) Will Garcia

68. Look at the graphic. How much did the man pay for the ticket?

(A) $5
(B) $10
(C) $15
(D) $20

69. What happened yesterday?

(A) A discount was offered.
(B) A competition was held.
(C) A notice was posted online.
(D) A class was canceled.

70. Why is the man unable to attend the festival on Sunday?

(A) He is going to meet with family.
(B) He has to go on a business trip.
(C) He has to prepare for a contest.
(D) He is going to conduct a workshop.

PART 4

Directions: In this part, you will listen to several short talks by a single speaker. These talks will not be printed and will only be spoken one time. For each talk, you will be asked to answer three questions. Select the best response and mark the corresponding letter (A), (B), (C), or (D) on your answer sheet.

71. Who is the speaker?

(A) A flight attendant
(B) A ticket agent
(C) An airline pilot
(D) A security guard

72. When will Flight 876 reach its destination?

(A) At 5:10 P.M.
(B) At 5:20 P.M.
(C) At 5:30 P.M.
(D) At 5:40 P.M.

73. What does the speaker suggest listeners do?

(A) Complete a document
(B) Choose an in-flight meal
(C) Report to an information desk
(D) Confirm a flight time

74. What is being advertised?

(A) A residential cleaning service
(B) An eco-friendly product line
(C) A new supermarket chain
(D) An innovative home appliance

75. What is supposed to happen in March?

(A) A marketing campaign will start.
(B) Samples will be given to customers.
(C) A product will be available in retail stores.
(D) Existing models will be replaced.

76. According to the speaker, what can listeners do online?

(A) Download a special coupon
(B) Find a store location
(C) Ask for a refund
(D) Make a purchase

77. What type of business does the speaker work for?

(A) An accommodation facility
(B) A catering company
(C) A law firm
(D) A real estate agency

78. Why does the speaker say, "But over 75 guests will be attending this event"?

(A) To approve a request
(B) To confirm a plan
(C) To indicate a problem
(D) To show excitement

79. What does the speaker ask the listener to do?

(A) Print a revised contract
(B) Call a party planner
(C) Provide an attendee list
(D) Visit an event venue

80. When will the heat wave begin?

(A) On August 5
(B) On August 6
(C) On August 7
(D) On August 8

81. What are listeners advised to do?

(A) Avoid exercise
(B) Park in designated areas
(C) Report health problems
(D) Contact an official

82. What does the speaker say is available on the Web site?

(A) Traffic updates
(B) Medical information
(C) Air quality data
(D) Nutrition tips

GO ON TO THE NEXT PAGE

83. What type of business is being advertised?

(A) An advertising firm
(B) An educational institution
(C) A financial company
(D) A recruitment agency

84. According to the speaker, why is the company highly ranked in a survey?

(A) Its services are inexpensive.
(B) Its managers are experienced.
(C) Its products are reliable.
(D) Its employees are trustworthy.

85. Why should listeners contact the hotline?

(A) To verify a payment
(B) To arrange a consultation
(C) To cancel a service
(D) To participate in a survey

---

86. Who most likely is the speaker?

(A) A technician
(B) A designer
(C) A secretary
(D) A telemarketer

87. What does the speaker mean when he says, "the problem is more serious than I thought"?

(A) A screen cannot be ordered.
(B) A phone is an outdated model.
(C) A device is significantly damaged.
(D) A component needs to be upgraded.

88. What does the speaker offer?

(A) A store credit
(B) A special discount
(C) A free product
(D) A warranty extension

---

89. What is the main purpose of the talk?

(A) To explain a company regulation
(B) To introduce a software product
(C) To discuss an insurance plan
(D) To promote a Web site

90. According to the speaker, what can managers do?

(A) Receive customer feedback
(B) Approve program updates
(C) Change staff assignments
(D) Track employee performance

91. What will most likely happen next?

(A) A video will be played.
(B) A demonstration will be given.
(C) A supervisor will be introduced.
(D) A questionnaire will be distributed.

Bretford Incorporated - Interview Dates	
Monday, May 2	Marketing Department
Tuesday, May 3	Design Department
Wednesday, May 4	Sales Department
Thursday, May 5	Accounting Department
Friday, May 6	No Interviews Scheduled

92. Look at the graphic. Which department is the woman applying to?

(A) Marketing
(B) Design
(C) Sales
(D) Accounting

93. What does the speaker ask the listener to do?

(A) Provide a job description
(B) Check on a delivery
(C) Change a schedule
(D) Expedite a process

94. What did the speaker do on Wednesday?

(A) Replied to an e-mail
(B) Submitted a sample
(C) Visited a family member
(D) Filled out an application

Staircase	Booth A	Booth B	
Ground Floor Bathroom		Booth C	Booth D	Information Desk

Dickson's Office Supply

$10 off any purchase over $40 in value
$20 off any purchase over $60 in value

Expires October 20

01234567890123

95. What is mentioned about the event?

(A) It has participants from many countries.
(B) It occurs in the same city every year.
(C) It is sponsored by local organizations.
(D) It will end later than expected.

96. Look at the graphic. Which booth is Matthew Walsh using?

(A) Booth A
(B) Booth B
(C) Booth C
(D) Booth D

97. According to the speaker, what can listeners do at the information desk?

(A) Pick up a brochure
(B) Buy a ticket
(C) Enter a contest
(D) Register for a class

98. Why does the speaker need to purchase furniture?

(A) A manager is being promoted.
(B) A department is changing offices.
(C) An employee is being transferred.
(D) A team is starting a new project.

99. Look at the graphic. How much of a discount will the company most likely receive?

(A) $10
(B) $20
(C) $40
(D) $60

100. What does the speaker say she will do?

(A) Reply to an e-mail
(B) Send a form
(C) Contact a supplier
(D) Drop by a store

解答 p.148 / 分數換算表 p.149 / 題目解析 p.373（解答本）

❚ 請翻到次頁的「自我檢測表」檢視自己解答問題的方法與態度。
❚ 請利用 p.149 分數換算表換算完分數。

1 2 3 4 5 6 7 8 9 10

自我檢測表

順利結束 TEST 09 了嗎？

現在透過以下問題來檢視一下自己的作答情況吧！

1. 我在作答時，中間沒有停下來過。
   □ 是　□ 否
   若答案為否，理由是為什麼呢？

2. 我有確實劃記答案紙上的每一道題目。
   □ 是　□ 否
   若答案為否，理由是為什麼呢？

3. 作答 Part 2 的 25 題時，我非常專心於題目上。
   □ 是　□ 否
   若答案為否，理由是為什麼呢？

4. 作答 Part 3 時，我在聽題目音檔前都已先看過題目和選項。
   □ 是　□ 否
   若答案為否，理由是為什麼呢？

5. 作答 Part 4 時，我在聽題目音檔前都已先看過題目和選項。
   □ 是　□ 否
   若答案為否，理由是為什麼呢？

6. 請寫下需要改進之處或給自己的建議。

★請確認自己在進行作答前寫下的目標分數，並再次堅定要達成目標的決心。需要改進的地方務必於下一回測驗中實踐，這一點非常重要，唯有如此才能更進步。

TEST 10

Part 1

Part 2

Part 3 新

Part 4 新

自我評量表

稍等！作答前確認事項：
1. 關掉手機電源了嗎？ □是
2. 準備好答案卡、鉛筆、橡皮擦了嗎？ □是
3. 準備好聽MP3了嗎？ □是

所有準備都完成後，請先預想目標成績，把它寫在
後面的自我檢測表上，再開始作答。

📱 **TEST 10.mp3** 收錄了 **Part 1-4**。

LISTENING TEST

In this section, you must demonstrate your ability to understand spoken English. This section is divided into four parts and will take approximately 45 minutes to complete. Do not mark the answers in your test book. Use the answer sheet that is provided separately.

PART 1

Directions: For each question, you will listen to four short statements about a picture in your test book. These statements will not be printed and will only be spoken one time. Select the statement that best describes what is happening in the picture and mark the corresponding letter (A), (B), (C), or (D) on the answer sheet.

Sample Answer
Ⓐ ● Ⓒ Ⓓ

The statement that best describes the picture is (B), "The man is sitting at the desk." So, you should mark letter (B) on the answer sheet.

1.

2.

GO ON TO THE NEXT PAGE

3.

4.

5.

6.

GO ON TO THE NEXT PAGE →

PART 2

Directions: For each question, you will listen to a statement or question followed by three possible responses spoken in English. They will not be printed and will only be spoken one time. Select the best response and mark the corresponding letter (A), (B), or (C) on your answer sheet.

7. Mark your answer on your answer sheet.

8. Mark your answer on your answer sheet.

9. Mark your answer on your answer sheet.

10. Mark your answer on your answer sheet.

11. Mark your answer on your answer sheet.

12. Mark your answer on your answer sheet.

13. Mark your answer on your answer sheet.

14. Mark your answer on your answer sheet.

15. Mark your answer on your answer sheet.

16. Mark your answer on your answer sheet.

17. Mark your answer on your answer sheet.

18. Mark your answer on your answer sheet.

19. Mark your answer on your answer sheet.

20. Mark your answer on your answer sheet.

21. Mark your answer on your answer sheet.

22. Mark your answer on your answer sheet.

23. Mark your answer on your answer sheet.

24. Mark your answer on your answer sheet.

25. Mark your answer on your answer sheet.

26. Mark your answer on your answer sheet.

27. Mark your answer on your answer sheet.

28. Mark your answer on your answer sheet.

29. Mark your answer on your answer sheet.

30. Mark your answer on your answer sheet.

31. Mark your answer on your answer sheet.

PART 3

Directions: In this part, you will listen to several conversations between two or more speakers. These conversations will not be printed and will only be spoken one time. For each conversation, you will be asked to answer three questions. Select the best response and mark the corresponding letter (A), (B), (C), or (D) on your answer sheet.

32. What problem are the speakers discussing?

   (A) A restaurant's interior is outdated.
   (B) A business is not attracting patrons.
   (C) There is not enough seating.
   (D) There are scratches on some tables.

33. What does the man suggest?

   (A) Removing a display container
   (B) Opening an outside seating area
   (C) Leasing some new machinery
   (D) Replacing some old chairs

34. What will the speakers most likely do this evening?

   (A) Shop for additional furniture
   (B) Put out some menus
   (C) Reorganize a space
   (D) Clean out a basement

35. Why is the woman calling the man?

   (A) To cancel a gathering
   (B) To ask about a service
   (C) To report an emergency
   (D) To respond to a message

36. What needs to be repaired?

   (A) A sidewalk
   (B) A road
   (C) A store's window
   (D) A building's roof

37. According to the man, what did a representative fail to do?

   (A) Fix part of a structure
   (B) Provide an estimate
   (C) Locate a property
   (D) Process a payment

38. According to the woman, what happened last Wednesday?

   (A) A team was assigned to a project.
   (B) A job posting was uploaded.
   (C) An administrator announced a policy change.
   (D) A staff member started in a new role.

39. When will a meeting begin?

   (A) At 3:00 P.M.
   (B) At 3:30 P.M.
   (C) At 4:00 P.M.
   (D) At 4:30 P.M.

40. What does the woman suggest?

   (A) Calling later
   (B) Accepting a job offer
   (C) Rescheduling an appointment
   (D) Checking trip details again

41. What concern does the woman mention?

   (A) Some equipment was not repaired.
   (B) A delivery did not arrive on schedule.
   (C) Insufficient items were ordered.
   (D) Workers were given faulty devices.

42. How many new computers are required for interns?

   (A) 5
   (B) 10
   (C) 15
   (D) 20

43. What task does the woman want carried out?

   (A) Downloading some manuals
   (B) Deleting some records
   (C) Speaking with a supervisor
   (D) Emptying out a storage closet

GO ON TO THE NEXT PAGE

44. Who most likely are the speakers?

    (A) Seminar organizers
    (B) Personal assistants
    (C) Emergency personnel
    (D) Maintenance staff

45. Why is the woman unable to help?

    (A) She is training another colleague.
    (B) She is no longer on duty.
    (C) She has to meet a deadline.
    (D) She is cleaning up a spill.

46. According to the man, what will happen this afternoon?

    (A) A meeting with the press will be held.
    (B) A lunch break will be postponed.
    (C) An office tour will be planned.
    (D) A lobby will undergo renovations.

47. What does the woman want to do?

    (A) Park at a residential complex
    (B) Purchase some equipment
    (C) Reserve a venue
    (D) Sign up for swimming lessons

48. What is mentioned about the facilities?

    (A) They will be cleaned in advance.
    (B) They are being redeveloped.
    (C) They are booked for a weekend.
    (D) They will be examined after use.

49. What does the man mean when he says, "There's a convenience store one block down Harvest Street"?

    (A) A shop offers competitive prices.
    (B) A retailer sells required supplies.
    (C) A building is easy to find.
    (D) A store branch has been moved.

50. Why has the man visited the woman's office?

    (A) To change an itinerary
    (B) To request a pamphlet
    (C) To pay some fees
    (D) To ask about insurance

51. What did the man recently do?

    (A) Visited a foreign country
    (B) Met with an adviser
    (C) Went to an event
    (D) Enrolled in a membership

52. What does the woman encourage the man to do?

    (A) Pay with a credit card
    (B) Call a different employee
    (C) Use a taxi service
    (D) Check nearby branch hours

53. What is the factory owner able to do?

    (A) Renew an annual contract
    (B) Arrange reasonable shipping rates
    (C) Increase a facility's output
    (D) Send sample products for free

54. Where will the man most likely conduct an inspection?

    (A) In India
    (B) In the United States
    (C) In Mexico
    (D) In Thailand

55. What did the woman do yesterday?

    (A) Revised a quality control report
    (B) Discovered a manufacturing defect
    (C) Participated in a videoconference
    (D) Approved a partnership agreement

56. What is the woman trying to do?

(A) Hire an accountant
(B) Submit a review
(C) Set up a service
(D) Relocate an office

57. Why does the man mention city zoning laws?

(A) To report a new regulation
(B) To justify denying a request
(C) To collect survey feedback
(D) To identify renovation costs

58. What will the woman most likely do next?

(A) Speak with a city official
(B) Read about a contractor
(C) Attend a neighborhood meeting
(D) Contact another company

---

59. What problem does Cathy inform Mr. Williams about?

(A) A job is no longer available.
(B) A document is missing.
(C) An exam has been canceled.
(D) An interview has to be postponed.

60. What does the woman mean when she says, "I think that will do it for me, Chris"?

(A) She wants Chris to explain benefits.
(B) She wants Chris to address a concern.
(C) She is not able to assist Chris.
(D) She is ready for Chris to end a meeting.

61. What will be sent by next Wednesday?

(A) An updated résumé
(B) Interview results
(C) Evaluation scores
(D) A lobby blueprint

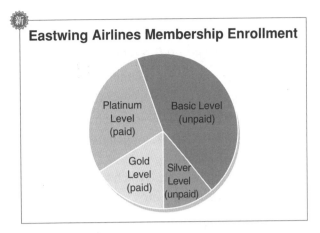

Eastwing Airlines Membership Enrollment

62. How can the woman find the codes?

(A) By looking through a manual
(B) By opening an e-mail attachment
(C) By accessing a Web site
(D) By checking a filing cabinet

63. Look at the graphic. Which level will the airline promote in the new advertisement?

(A) Basic Level
(B) Silver Level
(C) Gold Level
(D) Platinum Level

64. What does the man offer to do?

(A) Share a report
(B) E-mail some executives
(C) Duplicate some diagrams
(D) Analyze a marketing expense

GO ON TO THE NEXT PAGE

Azalea Apartments Building Directory	
2nd Floor	Laundry Room
3rd Floor	Fitness Center
4th Floor	Recreation Room
5th Floor	Management Office

65. Look at the graphic. Which floor are the speakers currently on?

(A) The 2nd Floor
(B) The 3rd Floor
(C) The 4th Floor
(D) The 5th Floor

66. Why is the gym closed today?

(A) Flooring is being removed.
(B) New machines are being installed.
(C) A tour is being conducted.
(D) Some damage is being repaired.

67. What does the woman imply about her colleague?

(A) He wants supplies for an office.
(B) He needs assistance with a device.
(C) He is having trouble locking a door.
(D) He will be late for an appointment.

Parking Lot Closed
May 6
Parking is available
at the Dalton Center Garage.

68. Who is Donald Powell?

(A) A department manager
(B) A construction worker
(C) A human resources intern
(D) A company president

69. Look at the graphic. Where will the sign most likely be placed?

(A) In a research laboratory
(B) In a factory
(C) In an administration office
(D) In a warehouse

70. What will the man distribute on May 1?

(A) Employee handbooks
(B) Facility maps
(C) Work schedules
(D) Parking passes

PART 4

Directions: In this part, you will listen to several short talks by a single speaker. These talks will not be printed and will only be spoken one time. For each talk, you will be asked to answer three questions. Select the best response and mark the corresponding letter (A), (B), (C), or (D) on your answer sheet.

71. What type of event will take place in February?

(A) A design contest
(B) A product launch
(C) A store opening
(D) A charity event

72. What does the speaker ask the listeners to do?

(A) Purchase winter outfits
(B) Select clothing items
(C) Assist with staff training
(D) Choose meal options

73. What will the speaker probably do later today?

(A) Review submissions
(B) Return to a mall
(C) Attend a fashion show
(D) Make an announcement

74. What is being advertised?

(A) A travel service
(B) A beach resort
(C) A residential remodeling company
(D) A real estate agency

75. What does the company specialize in?

(A) Hosting guests for long-term stays
(B) Providing housing loans
(C) Finding homes along a coastline
(D) Customizing interior designs

76. According to the speaker, how can listeners acquire more information?

(A) By calling a telephone number
(B) By sending an e-mail
(C) By filling in an online form
(D) By visiting an office

77. Why will a policy be changed?

(A) To address customer complaints
(B) To boost employee morale
(C) To promote the company's brand
(D) To improve workplace security

78. What does the speaker imply when he says, "but you don't have anything to worry about"?

(A) The yoga studio will reopen tomorrow.
(B) The uniform will be informal.
(C) The company logo will be popular.
(D) The staff will receive a present.

79. What does the speaker request that listeners do?

(A) Examine some documents
(B) Place an order with a supplier
(C) Write down some information
(D) Try on an outfit

80. According to the speaker, what can be found in the handbook?

(A) Some safety instructions
(B) A compensation policy
(C) Some contact information
(D) A list of work schedules

81. What will happen if staff submit daily reports more than a day late?

(A) They will have to write an explanatory note.
(B) They will have to resubmit some documentation.
(C) Their team leaders will notify them personally.
(D) Their yearly reviews will be affected.

82. According to the speaker, what should staff get permission for?

(A) Changing shifts with colleagues
(B) Working additional hours
(C) Accessing the accounting Web site
(D) Printing confidential records

GO ON TO THE NEXT PAGE

83. What does the speaker mention about the gift shop?

   (A) It has been shut down for renovations.
   (B) It is hosting a special event.
   (C) It is located near the South Gate.
   (D) It closes earlier than the main facility.

84. What does the speaker remind listeners about?

   (A) An exit is inaccessible.
   (B) A parking lot is full.
   (C) A storage area is available.
   (D) A center is open.

85. According to the speaker, what will happen next month?

   (A) A performance will be given.
   (B) A discount will be offered.
   (C) A temporary exhibit will be displayed.
   (D) An anniversary party will be held.

---

86. What is the report mainly about?

   (A) A public service
   (B) A workshop
   (C) A sponsorship program
   (D) A competition

87. What has Spencer Incorporated agreed to do?

   (A) Hire workers to clean the lake
   (B) Pay for participants' hotel costs
   (C) Supply awards for an event
   (D) Host a celebratory lunch

88. What does the speaker warn listeners about?

   (A) Weather complications
   (B) Road construction
   (C) Fishing permit modifications
   (D) Contest entrance fees

---

89. Where most likely do the listeners work?

   (A) At an advertising agency
   (B) At a convention center
   (C) At a financial institution
   (D) At a publishing firm

90. What does the man ask Derek to do?

   (A) Purchase equipment
   (B) Make a reservation
   (C) Contact a client
   (D) Distribute materials

91. 新 What does the speaker imply when he says, "Document Express printed the materials for our previous event in Ottawa"?

   (A) A printer made an error.
   (B) A promotion was successful.
   (C) A company should be hired again.
   (D) A brochure is not suitable for an event.

---

92. What is the speaker mainly discussing?

   (A) An employee orientation
   (B) A health program
   (C) A research project
   (D) An online discount

93. 新 Why does the speaker say, "You'll probably feel a lot better"?

   (A) To show agreement
   (B) To suggest a solution
   (C) To encourage participation
   (D) To confirm a decision

94. What does the speaker recommend that listeners do tomorrow?

   (A) Renew an identification card
   (B) Go to another building
   (C) Organize a workspace
   (D) Sign up for a membership

Flooring Type	Price per Square Meter
Tile	$20
Carpet	$25
Bamboo	$30
Hardwood	$35

Presswood Hotel Directory	
Housekeeping	5
Room Service	6
Front Desk	7
Concierge	8

95. Why is the speaker calling?

(A) To accept an offer
(B) To answer a question
(C) To request assistance
(D) To arrange a consultation

96. Look at the graphic. Which flooring type did the listener mention?

(A) Tile
(B) Carpet
(C) Bamboo
(D) Hardwood

97. According to the speaker, how can the listener get information about the materials?

(A) By going to a store
(B) By calling a hotline
(C) By visiting a Web site
(D) By sending an e-mail

98. According to the speaker, what will happen tomorrow?

(A) A facility will reopen.
(B) A pamphlet will be printed.
(C) A workshop will be held.
(D) A room will be renovated.

99. Look at the graphic. Which number should guests dial to request towels or pillows?

(A) 5
(B) 6
(C) 7
(D) 8

100. What will be offered to guests this week?

(A) Discounted tickets
(B) Free meals
(C) Gift bags
(D) Complimentary upgrades

解答 p.148 / 分數換算表 p.149 / 題目解析 p.417（解答本）

▌ 請翻到次頁的「自我檢測表」檢視自己解答問題的方法與態度。
▌ 請利用 p.149 分數換算表換算完分數。

自我檢測表

順利結束 TEST 10 了嗎？

現在透過以下問題來檢視一下自己的作答情況吧！

1. 我在作答時，中間沒有停下來過。

    ☐ 是　☐ 否

    若答案為否，理由是為什麼呢？

2. 我有確實劃記答案紙上的每一道題目。

    ☐ 是　☐ 否

    若答案為否，理由是為什麼呢？

3. 作答 Part 2 的 25 題時，我非常專心於題目上。

    ☐ 是　☐ 否

    若答案為否，理由是為什麼呢？

4. 作答 Part 3 時，我在聽題目音檔前都已先看過題目和選項。

    ☐ 是　☐ 否

    若答案為否，理由是為什麼呢？

5. 作答 Part 4 時，我在聽題目音檔前都已先看過題目和選項。

    ☐ 是　☐ 否

    若答案為否，理由是為什麼呢？

6. 請寫下需要改進之處或給自己的建議。

★請確認自己在進行作答前寫下的目標分數，並再次堅定要達成目標的決心。需要改進的地方務必
於下一回測驗中實踐，這一點非常重要，唯有如此才能更進步。

- 正確答案
- 分數換算表
- 答案紙
- 我的答錯
  題目筆記

正確答案 Answer Key

TEST 01

1 (B)	2 (C)	3 (C)	4 (A)	5 (D)
6 (B)	7 (B)	8 (C)	9 (A)	10 (B)
11 (C)	12 (A)	13 (C)	14 (A)	15 (B)
16 (C)	17 (B)	18 (C)	19 (A)	20 (C)
21 (A)	22 (A)	23 (B)	24 (B)	25 (A)
26 (C)	27 (B)	28 (C)	29 (B)	30 (B)
31 (A)	32 (D)	33 (A)	34 (C)	35 (A)
36 (C)	37 (A)	38 (B)	39 (B)	40 (A)
41 (A)	42 (D)	43 (B)	44 (C)	45 (D)
46 (A)	47 (D)	48 (C)	49 (D)	50 (C)
51 (D)	52 (C)	53 (C)	54 (D)	55 (A)
56 (C)	57 (D)	58 (B)	59 (D)	60 (C)
61 (B)	62 (D)	63 (C)	64 (D)	65 (D)
66 (A)	67 (C)	68 (D)	69 (A)	70 (A)
71 (A)	72 (D)	73 (B)	74 (D)	75 (D)
76 (B)	77 (C)	78 (D)	79 (B)	80 (A)
81 (D)	82 (A)	83 (C)	84 (D)	85 (B)
86 (D)	87 (B)	88 (A)	89 (D)	90 (A)
91 (C)	92 (D)	93 (C)	94 (A)	95 (D)
96 (D)	97 (C)	98 (B)	99 (C)	100 (D)

TEST 02

1 (D)	2 (C)	3 (A)	4 (C)	5 (D)
6 (C)	7 (C)	8 (B)	9 (B)	10 (B)
11 (B)	12 (C)	13 (C)	14 (B)	15 (B)
16 (A)	17 (A)	18 (C)	19 (A)	20 (C)
21 (C)	22 (C)	23 (A)	24 (B)	25 (C)
26 (C)	27 (C)	28 (C)	29 (A)	30 (B)
31 (A)	32 (C)	33 (A)	34 (C)	35 (C)
36 (B)	37 (B)	38 (A)	39 (D)	40 (C)
41 (A)	42 (C)	43 (D)	44 (D)	45 (B)
46 (A)	47 (D)	48 (A)	49 (D)	50 (C)
51 (A)	52 (A)	53 (B)	54 (C)	55 (B)
56 (D)	57 (C)	58 (B)	59 (B)	60 (D)
61 (C)	62 (D)	63 (A)	64 (C)	65 (D)
66 (D)	67 (C)	68 (C)	69 (B)	70 (A)
71 (D)	72 (D)	73 (C)	74 (D)	75 (D)
76 (A)	77 (B)	78 (A)	79 (C)	80 (A)
81 (C)	82 (D)	83 (C)	84 (D)	85 (B)
86 (D)	87 (C)	88 (A)	89 (D)	90 (C)
91 (C)	92 (B)	93 (D)	94 (B)	95 (C)
96 (B)	97 (B)	98 (D)	99 (B)	100 (A)

TEST 03

1 (A)	2 (C)	3 (B)	4 (D)	5 (A)
6 (B)	7 (B)	8 (C)	9 (A)	10 (C)
11 (B)	12 (A)	13 (B)	14 (C)	15 (A)
16 (B)	17 (C)	18 (B)	19 (B)	20 (C)
21 (B)	22 (B)	23 (A)	24 (B)	25 (C)
26 (A)	27 (C)	28 (B)	29 (A)	30 (A)
31 (A)	32 (B)	33 (D)	34 (D)	35 (C)
36 (A)	37 (A)	38 (D)	39 (B)	40 (C)
41 (D)	42 (A)	43 (B)	44 (C)	45 (D)
46 (D)	47 (C)	48 (C)	49 (B)	50 (C)
51 (B)	52 (B)	53 (C)	54 (D)	55 (A)
56 (A)	57 (D)	58 (B)	59 (B)	60 (C)
61 (B)	62 (A)	63 (C)	64 (B)	65 (C)
66 (B)	67 (C)	68 (C)	69 (C)	70 (B)
71 (B)	72 (D)	73 (A)	74 (B)	75 (C)
76 (D)	77 (A)	78 (C)	79 (A)	80 (A)
81 (B)	82 (C)	83 (A)	84 (B)	85 (C)
86 (D)	87 (B)	88 (D)	89 (C)	90 (D)
91 (D)	92 (B)	93 (A)	94 (C)	95 (C)
96 (A)	97 (A)	98 (A)	99 (D)	100 (C)

TEST 04

1 (C)	2 (D)	3 (A)	4 (D)	5 (C)
6 (C)	7 (C)	8 (C)	9 (B)	10 (C)
11 (B)	12 (C)	13 (A)	14 (B)	15 (A)
16 (B)	17 (B)	18 (C)	19 (C)	20 (A)
21 (B)	22 (C)	23 (A)	24 (B)	25 (A)
26 (C)	27 (B)	28 (B)	29 (B)	30 (C)
31 (A)	32 (B)	33 (C)	34 (A)	35 (D)
36 (C)	37 (B)	38 (A)	39 (D)	40 (D)
41 (C)	42 (A)	43 (A)	44 (B)	45 (C)
46 (A)	47 (C)	48 (D)	49 (B)	50 (B)
51 (A)	52 (C)	53 (A)	54 (D)	55 (B)
56 (C)	57 (A)	58 (D)	59 (A)	60 (B)
61 (C)	62 (D)	63 (B)	64 (D)	65 (A)
66 (C)	67 (A)	68 (C)	69 (B)	70 (B)
71 (C)	72 (D)	73 (B)	74 (D)	75 (A)
76 (B)	77 (C)	78 (A)	79 (B)	80 (D)
81 (C)	82 (D)	83 (B)	84 (D)	85 (A)
86 (B)	87 (A)	88 (C)	89 (C)	90 (A)
91 (B)	92 (B)	93 (C)	94 (A)	95 (C)
96 (B)	97 (A)	98 (D)	99 (B)	100 (C)

TEST 05

1 (B)	2 (A)	3 (B)	4 (D)	5 (C)
6 (A)	7 (C)	8 (B)	9 (A)	10 (B)
11 (C)	12 (B)	13 (B)	14 (A)	15 (A)
16 (B)	17 (B)	18 (B)	19 (A)	20 (A)
21 (A)	22 (B)	23 (C)	24 (C)	25 (C)
26 (A)	27 (C)	28 (A)	29 (C)	30 (A)
31 (B)	32 (B)	33 (C)	34 (A)	35 (C)
36 (A)	37 (D)	38 (C)	39 (A)	40 (C)
41 (D)	42 (A)	43 (A)	44 (C)	45 (A)
46 (C)	47 (D)	48 (C)	49 (D)	50 (A)
51 (D)	52 (A)	53 (C)	54 (D)	55 (D)
56 (D)	57 (C)	58 (B)	59 (B)	60 (D)
61 (A)	62 (B)	63 (A)	64 (A)	65 (B)
66 (A)	67 (D)	68 (B)	69 (C)	70 (A)
71 (A)	72 (B)	73 (B)	74 (A)	75 (D)
76 (C)	77 (D)	78 (D)	79 (B)	80 (A)
81 (D)	82 (C)	83 (D)	84 (B)	85 (B)
86 (C)	87 (A)	88 (A)	89 (C)	90 (A)
91 (D)	92 (C)	93 (A)	94 (D)	95 (A)
96 (A)	97 (B)	98 (D)	99 (C)	100 (B)

TEST 06

1 (C)	2 (D)	3 (A)	4 (B)	5 (B)
6 (C)	7 (C)	8 (B)	9 (A)	10 (A)
11 (A)	12 (C)	13 (C)	14 (B)	15 (C)
16 (C)	17 (B)	18 (C)	19 (C)	20 (A)
21 (C)	22 (C)	23 (A)	24 (B)	25 (C)
26 (B)	27 (A)	28 (C)	29 (C)	30 (A)
31 (C)	32 (B)	33 (D)	34 (A)	35 (B)
36 (A)	37 (B)	38 (D)	39 (D)	40 (B)
41 (C)	42 (D)	43 (A)	44 (C)	45 (A)
46 (D)	47 (C)	48 (D)	49 (B)	50 (A)
51 (D)	52 (C)	53 (B)	54 (C)	55 (A)
56 (B)	57 (C)	58 (B)	59 (A)	60 (B)
61 (D)	62 (D)	63 (A)	64 (B)	65 (B)
66 (C)	67 (A)	68 (D)	69 (C)	70 (B)
71 (A)	72 (B)	73 (D)	74 (C)	75 (B)
76 (A)	77 (C)	78 (C)	79 (D)	80 (D)
81 (A)	82 (A)	83 (B)	84 (A)	85 (D)
86 (C)	87 (D)	88 (B)	89 (B)	90 (C)
91 (D)	92 (A)	93 (B)	94 (C)	95 (D)
96 (B)	97 (A)	98 (A)	99 (C)	100 (B)

TEST 07

1 (C)	2 (A)	3 (D)	4 (D)	5 (A)
6 (B)	7 (C)	8 (B)	9 (A)	10 (B)
11 (C)	12 (B)	13 (B)	14 (C)	15 (A)
16 (C)	17 (B)	18 (C)	19 (A)	20 (B)
21 (B)	22 (C)	23 (A)	24 (C)	25 (C)
26 (B)	27 (C)	28 (A)	29 (B)	30 (B)
31 (B)	32 (A)	33 (B)	34 (D)	35 (C)
36 (B)	37 (C)	38 (B)	39 (A)	40 (D)
41 (B)	42 (A)	43 (A)	44 (B)	45 (C)
46 (D)	47 (C)	48 (C)	49 (B)	50 (C)
51 (D)	52 (A)	53 (C)	54 (D)	55 (A)
56 (D)	57 (C)	58 (B)	59 (C)	60 (A)
61 (C)	62 (D)	63 (D)	64 (B)	65 (D)
66 (A)	67 (D)	68 (C)	69 (A)	70 (C)
71 (C)	72 (D)	73 (A)	74 (B)	75 (C)
76 (D)	77 (C)	78 (A)	79 (B)	80 (C)
81 (B)	82 (A)	83 (B)	84 (B)	85 (C)
86 (D)	87 (C)	88 (B)	89 (C)	90 (B)
91 (A)	92 (C)	93 (B)	94 (A)	95 (B)
96 (B)	97 (C)	98 (C)	99 (D)	100 (B)

TEST 08

1 (C)	2 (B)	3 (A)	4 (D)	5 (A)
6 (D)	7 (A)	8 (B)	9 (C)	10 (B)
11 (A)	12 (A)	13 (C)	14 (C)	15 (C)
16 (A)	17 (A)	18 (B)	19 (C)	20 (C)
21 (B)	22 (A)	23 (B)	24 (A)	25 (B)
26 (A)	27 (C)	28 (B)	29 (A)	30 (B)
31 (B)	32 (D)	33 (A)	34 (A)	35 (D)
36 (C)	37 (D)	38 (B)	39 (A)	40 (D)
41 (A)	42 (C)	43 (C)	44 (B)	45 (A)
46 (C)	47 (B)	48 (A)	49 (B)	50 (A)
51 (D)	52 (C)	53 (B)	54 (B)	55 (C)
56 (A)	57 (D)	58 (B)	59 (B)	60 (C)
61 (D)	62 (B)	63 (D)	64 (A)	65 (C)
66 (D)	67 (B)	68 (A)	69 (B)	70 (D)
71 (D)	72 (A)	73 (C)	74 (B)	75 (C)
76 (C)	77 (D)	78 (A)	79 (C)	80 (D)
81 (B)	82 (A)	83 (C)	84 (B)	85 (A)
86 (C)	87 (A)	88 (C)	89 (B)	90 (C)
91 (A)	92 (D)	93 (A)	94 (C)	95 (C)
96 (C)	97 (B)	98 (B)	99 (D)	100 (A)

TEST 09

1 (B)	2 (A)	3 (B)	4 (D)	5 (C)
6 (C)	7 (A)	8 (C)	9 (C)	10 (C)
11 (B)	12 (C)	13 (B)	14 (A)	15 (A)
16 (B)	17 (B)	18 (C)	19 (A)	20 (B)
21 (C)	22 (A)	23 (C)	24 (C)	25 (B)
26 (A)	27 (B)	28 (B)	29 (C)	30 (A)
31 (C)	32 (B)	33 (D)	34 (B)	35 (C)
36 (B)	37 (A)	38 (C)	39 (C)	40 (A)
41 (B)	42 (C)	43 (D)	44 (C)	45 (A)
46 (D)	47 (A)	48 (D)	49 (C)	50 (D)
51 (B)	52 (D)	53 (B)	54 (A)	55 (C)
56 (A)	57 (C)	58 (A)	59 (C)	60 (D)
61 (B)	62 (B)	63 (C)	64 (C)	65 (B)
66 (B)	67 (A)	68 (B)	69 (C)	70 (A)
71 (C)	72 (B)	73 (A)	74 (B)	75 (C)
76 (D)	77 (C)	78 (C)	79 (D)	80 (B)
81 (A)	82 (B)	83 (C)	84 (D)	85 (B)
86 (A)	87 (C)	88 (A)	89 (B)	90 (D)
91 (B)	92 (B)	93 (C)	94 (B)	95 (A)
96 (A)	97 (D)	98 (C)	99 (A)	100 (B)

TEST 10

1 (C)	2 (D)	3 (B)	4 (D)	5 (B)
6 (D)	7 (A)	8 (C)	9 (B)	10 (A)
11 (B)	12 (C)	13 (B)	14 (A)	15 (C)
16 (B)	17 (B)	18 (A)	19 (B)	20 (C)
21 (A)	22 (A)	23 (A)	24 (C)	25 (A)
26 (C)	27 (B)	28 (C)	29 (A)	30 (C)
31 (B)	32 (C)	33 (A)	34 (C)	35 (D)
36 (D)	37 (B)	38 (D)	39 (A)	40 (A)
41 (C)	42 (D)	43 (B)	44 (D)	45 (B)
46 (A)	47 (C)	48 (D)	49 (B)	50 (D)
51 (C)	52 (C)	53 (B)	54 (A)	55 (C)
56 (C)	57 (B)	58 (D)	59 (B)	60 (D)
61 (B)	62 (C)	63 (C)	64 (A)	65 (A)
66 (B)	67 (B)	68 (A)	69 (C)	70 (D)
71 (D)	72 (B)	73 (A)	74 (D)	75 (C)
76 (A)	77 (D)	78 (B)	79 (C)	80 (C)
81 (D)	82 (B)	83 (D)	84 (A)	85 (C)
86 (D)	87 (C)	88 (B)	89 (A)	90 (B)
91 (C)	92 (B)	93 (C)	94 (D)	95 (B)
96 (D)	97 (C)	98 (A)	99 (C)	100 (B)

分數換算表

*請用以下的分數換算表來預測自己的多益聽力測驗成績。

答對題數	Listening	答對題數	Listening	答對題數	Listening
100	495	66	290	32	100
99	490	65	285	31	95
98	485	64	275	30	90
97	480	63	270	29	85
96	470	62	265	28	80
95	460	61	260	27	75
94	455	60	255	26	70
93	450	59	245	25	65
92	445	58	240	24	60
91	440	57	235	23	55
90	435	56	230	22	50
89	425	55	225	21	45
88	420	54	220	20	40
87	415	53	215	19	35
86	410	52	210	18	35
85	405	51	205	17	30
84	395	50	200	16	30
83	390	49	190	15	25
82	385	48	185	14	25
81	380	47	180	13	20
80	375	46	175	12	20
79	365	45	170	11	15
78	360	44	165	10	15
77	355	43	160	9	10
76	350	42	155	8	10
75	345	41	150	7	5
74	335	40	145	6	5
73	330	39	135	5	5
72	325	38	130	4	5
71	320	37	125	3	5
70	315	36	120	2	5
69	305	35	115	1	5
68	300	34	110	0	5
67	295	33	105		

Answer Sheet

TEST 02

LISTENING (Part I~IV)

答對題數：＿＿＿／100

換算 TEST 02 的成績後，請在目標設定評量表標記 TEST 02 的成績。
分數換算表在試題本的第149頁，目標設定評量表在試題本的第一頁。

✂ 裁切線

Answer Sheet

TEST 01

LISTENING (Part I~IV)

答對題數：＿＿＿／100

換算 TEST 01 的成績後，請在目標設定評量表標記 TEST 01 的成績。
分數換算表在試題本的第149頁，目標設定評量表在試題本的第一頁。

✂ 裁切線

Answer Sheet

TEST 04

LISTENING (Part I~IV)

	A B C D		A B C D		A B C D		A B C D		A B C D
1	Ⓐ Ⓑ Ⓒ Ⓓ	21	Ⓐ Ⓑ Ⓒ Ⓓ	41	Ⓐ Ⓑ Ⓒ Ⓓ	61	Ⓐ Ⓑ Ⓒ Ⓓ	81	Ⓐ Ⓑ Ⓒ Ⓓ
2	Ⓐ Ⓑ Ⓒ Ⓓ	22	Ⓐ Ⓑ Ⓒ Ⓓ	42	Ⓐ Ⓑ Ⓒ Ⓓ	62	Ⓐ Ⓑ Ⓒ Ⓓ	82	Ⓐ Ⓑ Ⓒ Ⓓ
3	Ⓐ Ⓑ Ⓒ Ⓓ	23	Ⓐ Ⓑ Ⓒ Ⓓ	43	Ⓐ Ⓑ Ⓒ Ⓓ	63	Ⓐ Ⓑ Ⓒ Ⓓ	83	Ⓐ Ⓑ Ⓒ Ⓓ
4	Ⓐ Ⓑ Ⓒ Ⓓ	24	Ⓐ Ⓑ Ⓒ Ⓓ	44	Ⓐ Ⓑ Ⓒ Ⓓ	64	Ⓐ Ⓑ Ⓒ Ⓓ	84	Ⓐ Ⓑ Ⓒ Ⓓ
5	Ⓐ Ⓑ Ⓒ Ⓓ	25	Ⓐ Ⓑ Ⓒ Ⓓ	45	Ⓐ Ⓑ Ⓒ Ⓓ	65	Ⓐ Ⓑ Ⓒ Ⓓ	85	Ⓐ Ⓑ Ⓒ Ⓓ
6	Ⓐ Ⓑ Ⓒ Ⓓ	26	Ⓐ Ⓑ Ⓒ Ⓓ	46	Ⓐ Ⓑ Ⓒ Ⓓ	66	Ⓐ Ⓑ Ⓒ Ⓓ	86	Ⓐ Ⓑ Ⓒ Ⓓ
7	Ⓐ Ⓑ Ⓒ Ⓓ	27	Ⓐ Ⓑ Ⓒ	47	Ⓐ Ⓑ Ⓒ Ⓓ	67	Ⓐ Ⓑ Ⓒ Ⓓ	87	Ⓐ Ⓑ Ⓒ Ⓓ
8	Ⓐ Ⓑ Ⓒ Ⓓ	28	Ⓐ Ⓑ Ⓒ	48	Ⓐ Ⓑ Ⓒ Ⓓ	68	Ⓐ Ⓑ Ⓒ Ⓓ	88	Ⓐ Ⓑ Ⓒ Ⓓ
9	Ⓐ Ⓑ Ⓒ Ⓓ	29	Ⓐ Ⓑ Ⓒ	49	Ⓐ Ⓑ Ⓒ Ⓓ	69	Ⓐ Ⓑ Ⓒ Ⓓ	89	Ⓐ Ⓑ Ⓒ Ⓓ
10	Ⓐ Ⓑ Ⓒ Ⓓ	30	Ⓐ Ⓑ Ⓒ	50	Ⓐ Ⓑ Ⓒ Ⓓ	70	Ⓐ Ⓑ Ⓒ Ⓓ	90	Ⓐ Ⓑ Ⓒ Ⓓ
11	Ⓐ Ⓑ Ⓒ Ⓓ	31	Ⓐ Ⓑ Ⓒ	51	Ⓐ Ⓑ Ⓒ Ⓓ	71	Ⓐ Ⓑ Ⓒ Ⓓ	91	Ⓐ Ⓑ Ⓒ Ⓓ
12	Ⓐ Ⓑ Ⓒ Ⓓ	32	Ⓐ Ⓑ Ⓒ	52	Ⓐ Ⓑ Ⓒ Ⓓ	72	Ⓐ Ⓑ Ⓒ Ⓓ	92	Ⓐ Ⓑ Ⓒ Ⓓ
13	Ⓐ Ⓑ Ⓒ Ⓓ	33	Ⓐ Ⓑ Ⓒ	53	Ⓐ Ⓑ Ⓒ Ⓓ	73	Ⓐ Ⓑ Ⓒ Ⓓ	93	Ⓐ Ⓑ Ⓒ Ⓓ
14	Ⓐ Ⓑ Ⓒ Ⓓ	34	Ⓐ Ⓑ Ⓒ	54	Ⓐ Ⓑ Ⓒ Ⓓ	74	Ⓐ Ⓑ Ⓒ Ⓓ	94	Ⓐ Ⓑ Ⓒ Ⓓ
15	Ⓐ Ⓑ Ⓒ Ⓓ	35	Ⓐ Ⓑ Ⓒ	55	Ⓐ Ⓑ Ⓒ Ⓓ	75	Ⓐ Ⓑ Ⓒ Ⓓ	95	Ⓐ Ⓑ Ⓒ Ⓓ
16	Ⓐ Ⓑ Ⓒ Ⓓ	36	Ⓐ Ⓑ Ⓒ	56	Ⓐ Ⓑ Ⓒ Ⓓ	76	Ⓐ Ⓑ Ⓒ Ⓓ	96	Ⓐ Ⓑ Ⓒ Ⓓ
17	Ⓐ Ⓑ Ⓒ Ⓓ	37	Ⓐ Ⓑ Ⓒ	57	Ⓐ Ⓑ Ⓒ Ⓓ	77	Ⓐ Ⓑ Ⓒ Ⓓ	97	Ⓐ Ⓑ Ⓒ Ⓓ
18	Ⓐ Ⓑ Ⓒ Ⓓ	38	Ⓐ Ⓑ Ⓒ	58	Ⓐ Ⓑ Ⓒ Ⓓ	78	Ⓐ Ⓑ Ⓒ Ⓓ	98	Ⓐ Ⓑ Ⓒ Ⓓ
19	Ⓐ Ⓑ Ⓒ Ⓓ	39	Ⓐ Ⓑ Ⓒ	59	Ⓐ Ⓑ Ⓒ Ⓓ	79	Ⓐ Ⓑ Ⓒ Ⓓ	99	Ⓐ Ⓑ Ⓒ Ⓓ
20	Ⓐ Ⓑ Ⓒ Ⓓ	40	Ⓐ Ⓑ Ⓒ	60	Ⓐ Ⓑ Ⓒ Ⓓ	80	Ⓐ Ⓑ Ⓒ Ⓓ	100	Ⓐ Ⓑ Ⓒ Ⓓ

答對題數： ＿＿＿ /100

換算 TEST 04 的成績後，請在目標設定評量表標記 TEST 04 的成績。
分數換算表在試題本的第149頁，目標設定評量表在試題本的第一頁。

✂ ---------- 裁切線

Answer Sheet

TEST 03

LISTENING (Part I~IV)

	A B C D		A B C D		A B C D		A B C D		A B C D
1	Ⓐ Ⓑ Ⓒ Ⓓ	21	Ⓐ Ⓑ Ⓒ Ⓓ	41	Ⓐ Ⓑ Ⓒ Ⓓ	61	Ⓐ Ⓑ Ⓒ Ⓓ	81	Ⓐ Ⓑ Ⓒ Ⓓ
2	Ⓐ Ⓑ Ⓒ Ⓓ	22	Ⓐ Ⓑ Ⓒ Ⓓ	42	Ⓐ Ⓑ Ⓒ Ⓓ	62	Ⓐ Ⓑ Ⓒ Ⓓ	82	Ⓐ Ⓑ Ⓒ Ⓓ
3	Ⓐ Ⓑ Ⓒ Ⓓ	23	Ⓐ Ⓑ Ⓒ Ⓓ	43	Ⓐ Ⓑ Ⓒ Ⓓ	63	Ⓐ Ⓑ Ⓒ Ⓓ	83	Ⓐ Ⓑ Ⓒ Ⓓ
4	Ⓐ Ⓑ Ⓒ Ⓓ	24	Ⓐ Ⓑ Ⓒ Ⓓ	44	Ⓐ Ⓑ Ⓒ Ⓓ	64	Ⓐ Ⓑ Ⓒ Ⓓ	84	Ⓐ Ⓑ Ⓒ Ⓓ
5	Ⓐ Ⓑ Ⓒ Ⓓ	25	Ⓐ Ⓑ Ⓒ Ⓓ	45	Ⓐ Ⓑ Ⓒ Ⓓ	65	Ⓐ Ⓑ Ⓒ Ⓓ	85	Ⓐ Ⓑ Ⓒ Ⓓ
6	Ⓐ Ⓑ Ⓒ Ⓓ	26	Ⓐ Ⓑ Ⓒ Ⓓ	46	Ⓐ Ⓑ Ⓒ Ⓓ	66	Ⓐ Ⓑ Ⓒ Ⓓ	86	Ⓐ Ⓑ Ⓒ Ⓓ
7	Ⓐ Ⓑ Ⓒ	27	Ⓐ Ⓑ Ⓒ Ⓓ	47	Ⓐ Ⓑ Ⓒ Ⓓ	67	Ⓐ Ⓑ Ⓒ Ⓓ	87	Ⓐ Ⓑ Ⓒ Ⓓ
8	Ⓐ Ⓑ Ⓒ	28	Ⓐ Ⓑ Ⓒ Ⓓ	48	Ⓐ Ⓑ Ⓒ Ⓓ	68	Ⓐ Ⓑ Ⓒ Ⓓ	88	Ⓐ Ⓑ Ⓒ Ⓓ
9	Ⓐ Ⓑ Ⓒ	29	Ⓐ Ⓑ Ⓒ Ⓓ	49	Ⓐ Ⓑ Ⓒ Ⓓ	69	Ⓐ Ⓑ Ⓒ Ⓓ	89	Ⓐ Ⓑ Ⓒ Ⓓ
10	Ⓐ Ⓑ Ⓒ	30	Ⓐ Ⓑ Ⓒ Ⓓ	50	Ⓐ Ⓑ Ⓒ Ⓓ	70	Ⓐ Ⓑ Ⓒ Ⓓ	90	Ⓐ Ⓑ Ⓒ Ⓓ
11	Ⓐ Ⓑ Ⓒ	31	Ⓐ Ⓑ Ⓒ Ⓓ	51	Ⓐ Ⓑ Ⓒ Ⓓ	71	Ⓐ Ⓑ Ⓒ Ⓓ	91	Ⓐ Ⓑ Ⓒ Ⓓ
12	Ⓐ Ⓑ Ⓒ	32	Ⓐ Ⓑ Ⓒ Ⓓ	52	Ⓐ Ⓑ Ⓒ Ⓓ	72	Ⓐ Ⓑ Ⓒ Ⓓ	92	Ⓐ Ⓑ Ⓒ Ⓓ
13	Ⓐ Ⓑ Ⓒ	33	Ⓐ Ⓑ Ⓒ Ⓓ	53	Ⓐ Ⓑ Ⓒ Ⓓ	73	Ⓐ Ⓑ Ⓒ Ⓓ	93	Ⓐ Ⓑ Ⓒ Ⓓ
14	Ⓐ Ⓑ Ⓒ	34	Ⓐ Ⓑ Ⓒ Ⓓ	54	Ⓐ Ⓑ Ⓒ Ⓓ	74	Ⓐ Ⓑ Ⓒ Ⓓ	94	Ⓐ Ⓑ Ⓒ Ⓓ
15	Ⓐ Ⓑ Ⓒ	35	Ⓐ Ⓑ Ⓒ Ⓓ	55	Ⓐ Ⓑ Ⓒ Ⓓ	75	Ⓐ Ⓑ Ⓒ Ⓓ	95	Ⓐ Ⓑ Ⓒ Ⓓ
16	Ⓐ Ⓑ Ⓒ	36	Ⓐ Ⓑ Ⓒ Ⓓ	56	Ⓐ Ⓑ Ⓒ Ⓓ	76	Ⓐ Ⓑ Ⓒ Ⓓ	96	Ⓐ Ⓑ Ⓒ Ⓓ
17	Ⓐ Ⓑ Ⓒ	37	Ⓐ Ⓑ Ⓒ Ⓓ	57	Ⓐ Ⓑ Ⓒ Ⓓ	77	Ⓐ Ⓑ Ⓒ Ⓓ	97	Ⓐ Ⓑ Ⓒ Ⓓ
18	Ⓐ Ⓑ Ⓒ	38	Ⓐ Ⓑ Ⓒ Ⓓ	58	Ⓐ Ⓑ Ⓒ Ⓓ	78	Ⓐ Ⓑ Ⓒ Ⓓ	98	Ⓐ Ⓑ Ⓒ Ⓓ
19	Ⓐ Ⓑ Ⓒ	39	Ⓐ Ⓑ Ⓒ Ⓓ	59	Ⓐ Ⓑ Ⓒ Ⓓ	79	Ⓐ Ⓑ Ⓒ Ⓓ	99	Ⓐ Ⓑ Ⓒ Ⓓ
20	Ⓐ Ⓑ Ⓒ	40	Ⓐ Ⓑ Ⓒ Ⓓ	60	Ⓐ Ⓑ Ⓒ Ⓓ	80	Ⓐ Ⓑ Ⓒ Ⓓ	100	Ⓐ Ⓑ Ⓒ Ⓓ

答對題數： ＿＿＿ /100

換算 TEST 03 的成績後，請在目標設定評量表標記 TEST 03 的成績。
分數換算表在試題本的第149頁，目標設定評量表在試題本的第一頁。

✂ 裁切線

Answer Sheet

TEST 06

LISTENING (Part I~IV)

換算 TEST 06 的成績後，請在目標設定評量表標記 TEST 06 的成績。目標設定評量表在試題本的第一頁
分數換算表在試題本的第149頁，

答對題數：＿＿／100

裁切線 ✂

Answer Sheet

TEST 05

LISTENING (Part I~IV)

換算 TEST 05 的成績後，請在目標設定評量表標記 TEST 05 的成績。目標設定評量表在試題本的第一頁
分數換算表在試題本的第149頁，

答對題數：＿＿／100

✂ **裁切線**